THE DIVING POOL

Yoko Ogawa has written more than twenty
works of fiction and non-fiction and has won
every major Japanese literary award. Her fiction
has appeared in the *New Yorker*, *A Public Space*
and *Zoetrope*.

YOKO OGAWA

The Diving Pool

TRANSLATED FROM THE JAPANESE BY
Stephen Snyder

VINTAGE BOOKS
London

Published by Vintage 2009

2 4 6 8 10 9 7 5 3 1

'Diving Pool' © Yoko Ogawa 1990

'Dormitory' and 'Ninshin Karenda/Pregnancy Diary' © Yoko Ogawa 1991
English translation copyright © Stephen Snyder 2008

Yoko Ogawa has asserted her right under the Copyright, Designs
and Patents Act 1988 to be identified as the author of this work

The Diving Pool first published in Japan by Fukutake Publishing Co., Ltd.
as *Samenai Koucha*.

Dormitory and *The Pregnancy Diary* first published in Japan by Bungei
Shunju Ltd. as *Ninshin Karenda*.

English translation rights arranged with Yoko Ogawa through Japan
Foreign-Rights Centre/ The Irene Skolnick Literary Agency

The English translation of *Pregnancy Diary* first appeared in slightly
different form in the *New Yorker* in 2005. The English translation of
The Diving Pool first appeared in Zoetrope in 2007.

First published in Great Britain in 2008 by
Harvill Secker

Vintage
Random House, 20 Vauxhall Bridge Road,
London SW1V 2SA

www.vintage-books.co.uk

Addresses for companies within The Random House Group Limited can
be found at: www.randomhouse.co.uk/offices.htm

The Random House Group Limited Reg. No. 954009

A CIP catalogue record for this book
is available from the British Library

ISBN 9780099521358

The Random House Group Limited supports The Forest Stewardship
Council (FSC), the leading international forest certification organisation.
All our titles that are printed on Greenpeace approved FSC certified paper
carry the FSC logo. Our paper procurement policy can be found at:
www.rbooks.co.uk/environment

Printed in the UK by CPI Bookmarque, Croydon, CR0 4TD

Contents

THE DIVING POOL

THE
DIVING
POOL

It's always warm here: I feel as though I've been swallowed by a huge animal. After a few minutes, my hair, my eyelashes, even the blouse of my school uniform are damp from the heat and humidity, and I'm bathed in a moist film that smells vaguely of chlorine.

Far below my feet, gentle ripples disrupt the pale blue surface of the water. A constant stream of tiny bubbles rises from the diving well; I can't see the bottom. The ceiling is made of glass and is very high. I sit here, halfway up the bleachers, as if suspended in midair.

Jun is walking out on the ten-meter board. He's

wearing the rust-colored swimsuit I saw yesterday on the drying rack outside the window of his room. When he reaches the end of the board, he turns slowly; then, facing away from the water, he aligns his heels. Every muscle in his body is tensed, as if he were holding his breath. The line of muscle from his ankle to his thigh has the cold elegance of a bronze statue.

Sometimes I wish I could describe how wonderful I feel in those few seconds from the time he spreads his arms above his head, as if trying to grab hold of something, to the instant he vanishes into the water. But I can never find the right words. Perhaps it's because he's falling through time, to a place where words can never reach.

"Inward two-and-a-half in the tuck position," I murmur.

He misses the dive. His chest hits the water with a smack and sends up a great spray of white.

But I enjoy it just the same, whether he misses a dive or hits it perfectly with no splash. So I never sit here hoping for a good dive, and I am never disappointed by a bad one. Jun's graceful body cuts through these childish emotions to reach the deepest place inside me.

He reappears out of the foam, the rippling surface of the water gathering up like a veil around his shoulders; and he swims slowly toward the side of the pool.

I've seen pictures from underwater cameras. The frame is completely filled with deep blue water, and then the diver shoots down, only to turn at the bottom and kick off back toward the surface. This underwater pivot is even more beautiful than the dive itself: the ankles and hands slice through the water majestically, and the body is completely enclosed in the purity of the pool. When the women dive, their hair flutters underwater as though lifted in a breeze, and they all look so peaceful, like children doing deep-breathing exercises.

One after the other, the divers come slipping into the water, making their graceful arcs in front of the camera. I would like them to move more slowly, to stay longer, but after a few seconds their heads appear again above the surface.

Does Jun let his body float free at the bottom of the pool, like a fetus in its mother's womb? How I'd love to watch him to my heart's content as he drifts there, utterly free.

I spend a lot of time on the bleachers at the edge of the diving pool. I was here yesterday and the day before, and three months ago as well. I'm not thinking about anything or waiting for something; in fact, I don't seem to have any reason to be here at all. I just sit and look at Jun's wet body.

We've lived under the same roof for more than ten years, and we go to the same high school, so we see each other and talk any number of times every day. But it's when we're at the pool that I feel closest to Jun— when he's diving, his body nearly defenseless in only a swimsuit, twisting itself into the laid-out position, the pike, the tuck. Dressed in my neatly ironed skirt and freshly laundered blouse, I take my place in the stands and set my schoolbag at my feet. I couldn't reach him from here even if I tried.

Yet this is a special place, my personal watchtower. I alone can see him, and he comes straight to me.

I pass the shops near the station and turn from the main road onto the first narrow street heading south, along the tracks. The noise and bustle die away. It's May now, and even when I reach the station after Jun's practice, the warmth of the day lingers in the air.

After I pass the park—little more than a sandbox and a water fountain—the company dormitory, and the deserted maternity clinic, there's nothing to see but rows of houses. It takes more than twenty-five minutes to walk home, and along the way the knot of people who left the station with me unravels and fades away with the sunlight. By the end, I'm usually alone.

A low hedge runs along the side of the road. It eventually gives way to trees, and then the cinder-block wall, half covered with ivy, comes into view. In the places where the ivy doesn't grow, the wall has turned moss green, as if the blocks themselves were living things. Then the gate, standing wide open, held back by a rusted chain that seems to prevent it from ever being closed.

In fact, I have never seen it closed. It's always open, ready to welcome anyone who comes seeking God in a moment of trouble or pain. No one is ever turned away, not even me.

Next to the gate is a glass-covered notice board with a neon light, and on it is posted the Thought for the Week: WHO IS MORE PRECIOUS? YOU OR YOUR BROTHER? WE ARE ALL CHILDREN OF GOD, AND YOU MUST NEVER TREAT YOUR BROTHER AS A STRANGER. Every Saturday afternoon, my father spends a long time looking through the Bible before carefully grinding ink on his stone and writing out this Thought. The smell of the ink permeates the old box where he keeps his brushes and grinding stone. He pours a few drops from the tiny water pot into the well of the stone, and then, holding the ink stick very straight, he grinds the stick into a dark liquid. Only when he finishes this long process does he finally dip his brush. Each gesture is done slowly, almost maddeningly so, as if he were performing a solemn ritual, and I am always careful to creep quietly past his door to avoid disturbing him.

Attracted to the neon light, countless tiny insects crawl on the notice board among my father's perfectly formed characters. At some point, evening has turned to night. The darkness inside the gate seems even thicker than outside, perhaps due to the dense foliage that grows within. Trees are planted at random along the wall, their branches tangled and overgrown. The front yard is covered in a thick jumble of weeds and flowers.

In this sea of green, two massive ginkgo trees stand out against the night sky. Every autumn, the children put on work gloves to gather the nuts. As the oldest, Jun climbs up on one of the thick branches and shakes the tree, and then the younger children run around frantically amid the hail of nuts and dried yellow leaves. Passing near the trees always makes me think of the soft skins surrounding the nuts, squashed like caterpillars on the soles of the children's shoes, and of the horrible odor they spread through the house.

To the left of the ginkgo trees is the church, and at an angle beyond, connected by a covered corridor, the building we call the Light House. This is my home.

The pale blue moisture I absorbed in the stands at the pool has evaporated by the time I reach here; my body is dry and hollow. And it is always the same: I can never simply come home the way other girls do. I find myself reading the Thought for the Week, passing through the gate, entering the Light House—and something always stops me, something always seems out of place.

Sometimes, as I approach, the Light House appears fixed and acute, while I, by contrast, feel vague and dim. At other times, I feel almost painfully clear and sharp, while the Light House is hazy. Either way, there is always something irreconcilable between the house and me, something I can never get past.

This was my home. My family was here. Jun, too. I remind myself of these facts each time I surrender to the curtain of green and open the door of the Light House.

When I try to put my memories in some kind of order, I realize that the earliest ones are the clearest and most indelible.

It was a brilliant morning in early summer. Jun and I were playing by the old well in the backyard. The well had been filled in long before and a fig tree planted over it. We must have been four or five years old, so it was soon after Jun had come to live at the Light House. His mother had been a chronic alcoholic, and he had been born out of wedlock, so one of our loyal parishioners had brought him to us.

I had broken off a branch from the fig tree and was

watching the opalescent liquid ooze from the wound. When I touched it, the sticky emission clung to my finger. I broke another branch.

"Time for milky!" I said to Jun.

I made him sit on my lap, and I wrapped an arm around his shoulders as I brought the branch to his lips. Nothing about Jun's body then hinted at the muscular form later shining in the transparent water of the pool. My arms remember only the softness of an ordinary small child. Like a baby at the breast, he pursed his lips and made little chirping sounds, even wrapping his hands around mine as if he were clutching a bottle. The milk of the fig had a bitter, earthy smell.

I felt myself suddenly overcome by a strange and horrible sensation. It might have been the fig milk or the softness of Jun's body bringing it on, but that seemed to be the beginning—though I suppose it's possible this terrible feeling took hold of me even earlier, before I was even born.

I broke a thicker branch with more milk and smeared it against his mouth. He knit his brow and licked his lips, and at that moment the sunlight becomes intensely bright, the scene blurs to white, and my oldest memory comes to an end.

Since that time, I've had many similar moments, and I can never hear the words "family" and "home" without feeling that they sound strange, never simply hear them and let them go. When I stop to examine them, though, the words seem hollow, seem to rattle at my feet like empty cans.

My father and mother are the leaders of a church, a place they say mediates between the faithful and their god. They also run the Light House, which is an orphanage where I am the only child who is not an orphan, a fact that has disfigured my family.

Occasionally, perhaps to stir up this feeling that haunts me, I open one of the photo albums that line the bottom shelf of the bookcase in the playroom. I sit on the floor, amid the picture books and blocks, and select an album at random.

The photos were all taken at Light House events—picnics under the cherry blossoms, clam digging at low tide, barbecues, gathering ginkgo nuts—and every one is full of orphans. As in pictures from a class field trip, the faces are lined up one next to the other. And there I am, lost among them. If it were really a field trip, it would end; but these orphans came home with me to the Light House.

More often than not, my mother and father stand smiling behind the children. My father's smile is calm and even, and perhaps a bit perfunctory. Though that's to be expected for a man who spends half his life presiding over religious services and church functions. He is almost always praying his endless prayers. I gaze at the photograph of my father just as someone might gaze at the altar from the pew.

I flip sadly through an album, studying the photos. Each one is just like all the others, but none of them records my weight or length at birth, or contains a copy of my tiny footprint, or a picture of my parents and me. I slam it closed.

Sometimes I have thought it might be better if I were an orphan, too. If I could have one of the tragic histories so common at the Light House—an alcoholic mother, a homicidal father, parents lost to death or abandonment, anything at all—then I would have been a proper orphan. Then, like all the other children, I might have imagined that the nice couple who ran the Light House were my real parents, or pretended to be sweet and innocent in the hope of being adopted. Somehow, that would have made my life much simpler.

From the time of the incident with the fig tree, I wanted only one thing: to be part of a normal, quiet family.

Still, when Jun disappears into the locker room and I gather up my schoolbag, watching as the surface of the pool becomes calm and glasslike again, or, on Sunday nights, when I listen quietly for the sound of Jun coming home through the green darkness after a diving meet—at such times I feel my desire for a family evaporate like the mist.

I grope after it, though I know it's pointless. There are so many useless things in this world, but for me, the most useless of all is the Light House.

Jun came home. He had a meeting after practice, so he was an hour behind me.

Once a week or so, I managed to guess when he'd show up, and then I'd be waiting for him, casually perched on the couch or standing near the telephone in the hall. If the children or the staff or my parents—or most of all Jun himself—had realized that I was waiting for him, things would have been terribly complicated, so I was careful to make my presence seem accidental. I felt ridiculous, but I kept to my post, making pointless calls to school friends or flipping through magazines.

The front hall was usually quiet and empty in the evening. It is a plain room, with nothing but a frayed sofa and an old-fashioned telephone. The floorboards have a yellowish cast under the bare lightbulb.

This evening, I gave myself permission to wait for Jun. He came through the door, dressed in his school blazer and carrying his backpack and gym bag.

"Hello," I said.

"Hi." Even the most ordinary words seemed to move me when they came from Jun's mouth. The fresh, clean smell of the pool clung to his body, and his hair was still slightly damp, the way I loved to see it.

"I'm starved," he said, dropping his bags and slumping onto the sofa. But even this was done in a good-natured way, and his exhaustion was scented with the bright smell of the pool.

"I envy you," I said, leaning against the telephone stand. "You work up an appetite. But I do almost nothing and still eat three meals a day. There's something pointless about that sort of hunger."

"You should take up a sport," he said.

I shook my head without looking up. "I'd rather watch," I said, wincing at my own words.

Those hours at the pool were my private indulgence, and I made a point of sitting as far as possible from the diving platform in order to keep them secret. I was also careful to avoid running into Jun or his teammates at the entrance to the gym, so it was possible that he'd never realized I was there. Still, it made me sad somehow if he hadn't, even though I was the one taking all those precautions.

He'd never put me on the spot by telling me he'd seen me, or by asking what I was doing at the pool. But I felt our bond would be somehow stronger if he knew and had made a point of letting me go on.

"I hurt my wrist today," he said. "I must have hit the water at a funny angle."

"Which one?"

He shook his left wrist to show me. Because his body was so important to me, I lived in fear that he would injure it. The flash in his eyes as he was about to dive, the glint of light on his chest, the shapes of his muscles—it all aroused in me a pleasant feeling that usually lay dormant.

"Are you all right? The preliminaries for the inter-high meet are coming up, aren't they?"

"It's not serious," he said, leaving it at that.

To enter the pool like a needle, creating the least possible splash, Jun had to align his wrists perfectly at the instant he hit the surface of the water. Because he had been diving for so long, he had the strongest wrists I'd ever seen.

Just then, we heard the sound of slippers along the corridor, and Naoki ran into the room.

"Hi, Jun! Could you do a handstand?" He danced around Jun like an excited puppy. He was three years old and suffered from asthma, which left his voice hoarse.

"Okay, but not right now," Jun said, rising from the couch and catching Naoki in his arms. The children at the Light House loved Jun, perhaps because he was extraordinarily good to them. They loved him just

as I loved him, and everyone seemed to want to touch
him. As he headed off, Naoki still in his arms, I whispered that he should take care of his wrist.

"Then when?" Naoki whined. "And you have to
walk on your hands, too." The rough sound of his voice
disappeared down the hall.

To my mind, dinner was the strangest part of life at
the Light House—beginning with the fact that the
kitchen and the dining room are in the basement.

The church and the Light House are old, Western-
style wooden buildings, their age apparent in every
floorboard, hinge, and tile. The structures have become quite complex through frequent additions, and
from the outside it is impossible to grasp their layout.
Inside, they are more confusing still, with long, wind-
ing halls and small flights of stairs.

The foyer of the Light House leads to a maze of corridors that snake through the building and eventually
to a hall on the second floor that looks down on the
courtyard through a window. At the end of the hall,
there is a trapdoor in the floor with a heavy iron handle.
The door makes a dry creak when it's lifted. We would
fasten it to a hook on the ceiling before going down the
steep flight of stairs to the dining room and the kitchen.

The children loved the secret staircase. Before every meal there was a race—often ending in a fight—to see who could get to the trapdoor first. The director or one of the teachers hurried the children along as they disappeared down the staircase, one after the other.

When I pulled on the rusty handle, heard the creaking of the trapdoor, and smelled the odors of the kitchen coming up the stairs, I was often reminded of *The Diary of Anne Frank*: the stairs hidden behind the revolving bookcase, the plan of the secret house as convoluted as that of the Light House, the yellow Star of David, the pins in the map tracking the advancing invasion of Normandy, the gloomy, inadequate meals with Peter, the van Daans, and Dr. Dussel. Like Anne, I could feel my appetite diminish with each step I took down the secret stairs of the Light House.

Though the kitchen and dining room are partially underground, they were neither dark nor damp. There are a number of large windows overlooking the garden to the south, and from the windows to the north, light filters in through the woods.

Yet here, too, there were inescapable signs of age and decay. The frying pans and pots lined up on the drying rack were scorched and discolored, and the appliances—mixers, ovens, refrigerators, and the like—were sturdy but old. The surface of the enormous table that dominated the room was covered with scratches and, in places, hollowed out by deep gouges.

I found breakfasts in this dining room almost unbearable, amid a crowd of noisy children and scraps of scattered food. At dinnertime, my father, who went to bed early in order to be up for morning services, would eat with the dozen or so younger children; and afterward I would eat with Jun, Reiko, who was in the third year of middle school, the night proctor, and my mother. But even among the adults, after the tables had been wiped of the children's spills, I still found the meals disgusting.

My mother was the heartiest, most cheerful person at the Light House. Particularly talkative during dinner, she was not one to cast about for topics that would include everyone, preferring to talk about herself and her interests from the moment we sat down until the meal was over. As she would grow increasingly excited and out of breath, I often wondered whether she in fact hated herself for talking so much.

Eventually I began worrying that Jun and the others were growing weary of her. Her lips were like two maggots that never stopped wriggling, and I found myself wanting to squash them between my fingers. It was pitch black outside and the glass in the windows had turned a deep shade of green, but her voice tumbled brightly on in the darkening world. Reiko and the night proctor stared down at their plates and mumbled acknowledgments from time to time.

Jun's hair was dry by then. His body seemed smaller and more vulnerable when it wasn't wet. Unlike the rest of us, he never looked bored or sighed when my mother talked too much. Instead, he listened intently to her overbearing voice, nodding politely, eating with gusto, and even breaking in from time to time to ask a strategic question that encouraged her to talk even more. His voice seemed to blend with hers, and she turned to face him as her babbling grew more and more frantic.

Meanwhile, I sat studying his profile, wondering how he could be so kind while I felt nothing but the cruelest sort of disgust. He would come down from the diving board and return to the Light House, where his muscles would warm and soften like silk floss, and then he would soak up all the things that set my nerves on edge—Naoki's raspy voice, the scraps of food flung about by the children, my mother's endless chattering. It seemed strange that he could be so good when life had treated him so badly: a father who ran off when he was born and a mother who had abandoned him for the bottle. I prayed desperately to be bathed in his kindness.

The sound of children's feet came through the floor from upstairs. It was bath time: I could imagine them running around in great clouds of talcum powder. I stared at my mother's glistening lips and nudged my chopsticks against the fatty bits of meat left on my plate. Then I passed a sauce bottle to Jun, hoping to hear him say "Thank you"—the sound of his voice could wash away the sour feeling in my stomach.

It was a quiet Sunday afternoon. My mother and father had gone out to record a radio program for the church. Reiko, who shared my room, was stretched out on the top bunk reading a science magazine. Jun was at the ballet class he attended every week. He had started recently at the urging of his diving coach, who said it would help him with form and flexibility. I have trouble imagining him at ballet class, accustomed as I am to seeing his body framed in sparkling water at diving practice, but I found myself feeling jealous of those flat-chested little girls in white leotards, their hair pulled back in tight buns.

In Jun's absence, these Sunday afternoons seemed somber and endless. I kept busy by reviewing for my English class; when I became bored, I flipped through the dictionary at random, studying the simple yet strangely realistic illustrations: an albatross, a still, a wood box, a waffle iron.

It was a beautiful day outside. Sunlight covered the ground like a shower of gold dust. The shadows of trembling ginkgo leaves were etched sharply on the wall of the church, and the breeze blowing through the curtains carried the first hints of summer.

"Are you going to the hospital today?" I said, turning toward Reiko.

"No, not today," she replied without looking up from her magazine.

Reiko had come to the Light House less than six months earlier. My parents had carried in boxes stuffed with books and tired, out-of-fashion clothes, and then Reiko herself had appeared at the door of my room. She was heavyset and taller than I was, and she wore thick glasses. Though she was only in middle school, her flesh seemed to sag in places, like the body of a middle-aged woman.

"Pleased to meet you," she said, lumbering into the room as if her body were a burden.

It was rare for someone as old as Reiko to come to the Light House. Most children were brought as infants and were adopted while they were still young. Jun was the first to reach high school age while still living here.

Reiko's parents were both in a mental hospital. Their problems were apparently very serious, with no hope that they would recover and return to normal life.

"They'll miss you if you don't go." I knew that she didn't like talking about her parents, but I brought them up as often as possible. The children here suffered from almost every imaginable misfortune, yet it struck me as particularly bad luck to have both parents go crazy, one after the other.

"I wish they would miss me," she said. Closing the magazine, she sat up on the bed and took off her glasses. "I'd be glad if they did." With her glasses off, her eyes were so small it was hard to tell where she was looking.

"And that's what makes you so sad?" I asked.

She blinked nervously but said nothing. Her vacant stare confounded my efforts to understand what she was feeling. Her lips were pursed in what might have been a faint smile, but it might also have been a wounded frown. There were several seconds of icy silence.

"The hooks have come undone," she said at last, as if talking to herself.

"Hooks?"

"That's right. The ones that kept my mother and father and me together. They've come undone and there's no way to get them fastened again." Sometimes she spoke like a young lady from a good family.

I wondered what sort of sound was made when the

hooks holding together a family came apart. Perhaps a dull splat, like the sound of a ripe fruit splitting open. Or maybe it was more like an explosion, when you mix the wrong chemicals.

Reiko was still looking down at me blankly, the fat on her cheeks and chin hiding her feelings. She put her glasses on again, stretched out on the bed, and went back to her magazine.

Perhaps the wounds she'd received when the hooks broke were still raw. But since I'd never been hooked to anything, I couldn't see much difference in our luck.

I turned back to the desk and began writing unintelligible English words in my notebook. The children were even louder now, but their noise had no effect on the silence that fell between us.

The Light House was always noisy: a mixture of shouting and crying and pounding feet filled every corner of the building like some resident spirit.

Just then, an urgent knock sounded at the door, and the part-time nurse came in carrying Rie in her arms.

"We're going to take the children to the bazaar at the church, but Rie seems to be coming down with a cold. Could we leave her here with you?" She spoke quickly, rocking the child in her arms.

"Sure," I said, getting up from the desk to take Rie. "I'll look after her."

"Do you want to go with us, Reiko?" the nurse said, looking toward the top bunk.

"It's very kind of you to invite me, but I'm afraid I have other things I have to do today." As always, Reiko's refusal was excessively polite.

At a year and five months, Rie was the youngest child at the Light House. She wore a bright red play-suit over her white shirt, and her nose was shiny and damp.

The din from the children reached a crescendo and then subsided as they left with the three nurses. I took Rie downstairs and out in the backyard.

The brilliant sunlight made the shadowy places seem fresh and clean, and the objects in them—a tri-cycle, a broken flowerpot, every leaf and weed—stood out vividly. Cases of bottles waiting to be recycled and an empty box with a picture of asparagus were piled by the kitchen door.

After the fig tree had stopped bearing fruit, it was cut down, leaving only a small mound of earth where the well had been. Rie was amusing herself by stick-ing a little shovel into this mound while I watched from a short way off, seated on one of the cases of bottles.

The tiny legs protruding from the elastic hems of her pants looked like pats of smooth, white butter. Whether they are dark and blotchy, covered in a rash, or rippling with rings of fat, I am always fascinated by a baby's thighs. There is something almost erotic about their defenselessness, and yet they seem fresh and vivid, like separate living creatures.

Rie was scooping up dirt with the shovel she held in one hand and dumping it into the bucket she held in the other. She had been doing this for some time, but when she missed the bucket and spilled the dirt on her hand, she came staggering toward me on unsteady little legs, crossing the boundary between bright sunlight and quiet shade. She made little pleading noises as she held out her soiled hand. It seemed clean enough to me, but I blew on her palm anyway.

Children Rie's age have a peculiar odor: the dustiness of disposable diapers mixed with the pulpy smell of baby food. But in Rie's case, there was an added scent, like fresh butter at the moment you peel away the foil wrapper.

She went back to her game, yet every few minutes she would stop and come over to have me dust off her hands. The simple regularity with which she did this gradually put me in a cruel mood. However, I didn't find the feeling particularly unpleasant; in fact, there was something agreeable about it. This cruel impulse had been coming over me quite often then. It seemed to be concealed somewhere in the spaces between my ribs, and the strange baby smell brought it out, almost as though plucking it from my body. The pain of its emergence comforted me as I stood watching Rie.

Then, while she had her back turned, I slipped behind the kitchen door. After a few moments, the dirt on her hands began to bother her again and she dropped the shovel and bucket at her feet and stood staring at her palms. Finally, she turned for help toward the spot where I should have been sitting. As it dawned on her that I wasn't there, that she'd been left alone, she began crying in earnest. Her sobs were violent, seemingly about to rupture something inside her, and they were satisfying my cruel urge. I wanted her to cry even harder, and everything seemed perfectly arranged: no one would come to pick her up, I would be able to listen to my heart's content, and she was too young to tell anyone afterward.

When we grow up, we find ways to hide our anxieties, our loneliness, our fear and sorrow. But children hide nothing, putting everything into their tears, which they spread liberally about for the whole world to see. I wanted to savor every one of Rie's tears, to run my tongue over the damp, festering, vulnerable places in her heart and open the wounds even wider.

A dry breeze tugged at her straggly hair. The sun was still high in the sky, as if it were no longer setting, as if time had stopped. She continued to sob violently, barely able to catch her breath.

When I finally appeared from behind the door, she wailed even louder and came running to throw herself in my arms, her buttery little thighs churning all the way. As I lifted her up and held her, the sobs subsided into pitiful whimpers that barely hinted at her vanished anger. Damp with tears and snot, the little cheeks pressed against my chest, and with them came that strange child smell. The arrogance of Rie's self-assurance restored my cruel thoughts.

My eyes wandered to the large urn abandoned at the edge of the woods in back. Once a decoration in a hall at the Light House, it was a Bizen pot, nearly as tall as a man's chest. I carried Rie to it, rubbing her back to quiet her ragged breathing. Then I removed its lid of rotting boards and slowly lowered her inside.

I wanted to hear her cry louder. I wanted to hear every kind of howl or sob she could produce. Her legs contracted in terror, as if she were going into convulsions, and she clung to my arms.

"It's all right," I said, shaking off her tiny fingers. "Don't be afraid."

Inside, the urn was cool and damp. She flailed about, screaming at the top of her lungs. Her cries came pouring up and into me like a stream of molten steel. I gripped the mouth of the urn with both hands to keep it from toppling over and stared down at Rie's futile struggles.

Every day of my life I had heard someone crying at the Light House. In the brief pauses between rough-housing and fights, between laughter and screaming, there had always been tears. And I had tried my best to love every one of them because I was the orphan no family wanted to adopt, the only one who could never leave the Light House. Still, Rie's terrified tears were particularly satisfying, like hands caressing me in exactly the right places—not vague, imaginary hands but his hands, the ones I was sure would know just how to please me.

"Just a little more," I said, the words disappearing into the urn. As I watched her reach imploringly for me, my chin resting on the rim, I felt a giggle welling up inside.

I had been asleep for some time that night when suddenly I woke. The room wasn't hot, nor had I had a bad dream. Still, I was immediately awake and alert, as if I'd never slept, as if I were shining brightly in the darkness.

It was so quiet I thought I could hear the children breathing next door. Reiko seemed to be sleeping peacefully, and the springs groaned as she turned heavily in bed. I took the alarm clock from the bedside table and held it close to my face: 2:00 A.M. I'd slept just two hours, but I felt refreshed. It seemed impossible that morning was still far off.

Then, in the darkness and silence, I heard the faint sound of running water—so faint I suspected it might disappear altogether if I stopped listening. As I lay in bed picturing this stream, my mind became calm and clear.

I got up and looked out the window. The world was still; everything seemed to be asleep—the ginkgo tree, the Thought for the Week, the rusted chain on the gate—except for the water in the distance. I slipped quietly out of the room, following the sound.

The upstairs hall was dark, lit only by the bare bulb on the landing. The doors to the children's rooms were tightly shut. The floor was cool against my feet.

As I descended the stairs, the sound grew more distinct. I stood at the end of the longest hall in the Light House, the one that led to the underground dining room, and spied Jun at the sink across from the bathroom, washing his swimsuits under one of the four faucets.

"What are you doing up so late?" I said, staring at his wet, soapy hands.

"Sorry, did the noise wake you?" Even here in the

dark, in the middle of the night, his voice was clean and sharp. "For some reason, when I'm washing my suits and the house is still, I can think about diving."

"About diving?"

"I go over the dives in my head—the approach, the timing of the bounce, the entrance." His hands went on with their work as he talked. "If you picture a perfect dive over and over in your head, then when you get up on the board you feel as though you can actually do it." He washed the suits carefully, turning them inside out and rubbing them against the tiles in the sink. I loved the look of his fingers, moving so vigorously. When I was with him, I found myself wondering how he could be so pure and innocent.

"You love to dive, don't you?" I couldn't think of anything else to say.

"I do," he said. Two words, but they echoed inside me. If I could have just those two words all to myself, I felt I would be at peace. "When I'm diving I get completely absorbed in the moment—at least for those few tenths of a second." There was no doubt that Jun suspended in midair, from the time he left the board to the time he entered the water, was the most exquisite embodiment of him, as if all his good words and deeds were wrapped around his beautiful body and left to fall free through the air.

We stood in our pajamas, our images reflected in the line of mirrors above the sink. The house was utterly still, as if only the air around us were alive. The light, too, seemed to have collected on us; everything else beyond the windowpane and down the hall was pitch black. We inhabited some separate, extraordinary moment in time.

Jun had splashed water on his pajamas, and I could see the muscles of his chest even through the loose material. I felt like a weepy child, longing to be enfolded in his arms.

"Let me help you," I said, forcing myself to sound cheerful, afraid that unless I spoke I would be crushed by desire.

"Thanks," he said. I turned on the faucet next to him and rinsed the soap from one of the suits. I let the water trickle in a thin stream, cautious not to make noise and wake someone else, ending this moment with Jun. There were three suits, and I knew the pattern on each: the one he got when he first joined the diving team, the one from a big meet the previous year, the one the children had given him for his birthday. I knew them all by heart.

As I stood with my hands submerged in the water, feeling Jun next to me, I had a deep sense of peace. Perhaps it was the pleasure of holding something that had been so close to him. I thought back to a time when we were younger and could play together innocently, a time when Jun's body held no particular significance for me.

"Do you remember the day we had snow here in the hallway?" I asked, staring at the soap bubbles as they slid down the tiles.

"Snow? Here in the hall?" He turned to look at me.

"It was about ten years ago. I'd had a wonderful dream, and I woke up early. When I looked outside, everything was covered with snow, more than I'd ever seen. The children were still asleep. I jumped out of bed and ran downstairs, and the hall was completely buried in snow from one end to the other."

"Really? But why would there have been snow in the house?"

"It blew in through the cracks in the roof. The repairman came after the snow melted to nail boards over the holes. You really don't remember?"

Jun looked thoughtful for a moment. "I suppose it does sound vaguely familiar."

"Try to remember," I said. "It would be a shame to forget something so beautiful. The best part was seeing the hall before anyone came along to make footprints."

I finished rinsing the suit and set it on the ledge above the sink. Then Jun handed me the next one.

"It was amazing. I just stood there feeling like I was the only one awake in the whole world. But I wasn't; someone else was looking at the snow."

"Who?" I could feel his eyes on me.

"You. At some point I realized you were standing behind me, and I had the feeling you'd been there all along. You were wearing those blue pajamas with bees and bear cubs."

Jun's hands stopped moving for a moment. "And yours were polka dots," he said.

"That's right. We stood there, just the two of us— like we are now." I put the second suit next to the first one.

The memory of the soft snow—another extraordinary moment we had shared long before—came back to me through the soles of my feet. It had seemed like a dream, far removed from reality, and yet there had been something amazingly vivid about the snow and being there with Jun. I remember being delighted to be alone in that special place, just the two of us; but I'm sure it must have been even more wonderful then, when we were young and knew nothing about the pain of growing up.

"You said we should dive into it," I continued. "I was afraid, but you said it was safe, that it would be wonderful—and then you spread out your arms and fell in. You left a perfect print of yourself in the snow—we couldn't stop laughing, but we were quiet, so no one else would know. Then you pushed me in and I got snow all in my eyes."

"It was fun, wasn't it?" He sounded as though he would never know that sort of pleasure again. And perhaps he was right. It was hard to know what was coming, where our lives would lead, and it made me sad to think about the future.

I doubted that we would ever have a quiet chat about the night we washed out his swimsuits. One after the other, the children at the Light House all went away, leaving me behind. I had no idea how many of them I had watched go, standing alone at the window of my room; and there was no reason to believe that Jun wouldn't leave like the rest. One day he would go, dressed in his new clothes, accompanied by his new family, disappearing around the corner where the Thought for the Week was posted. And that was why I wanted to remember the happiness we'd had together while we still could.

I washed the suits with great care, as if by doing so I could wash away my cruelty to Rie that afternoon. I needed to pretend to be myself at a younger, more innocent age, when we had stood marveling at the snow in the hall. I was sure that Jun would dive into only pure water, and I wanted his dive into me to be perfect; I wanted him to enter with no splash at all.

Once we'd finished talking about that morning so many years before, we couldn't think of anything else to say. The sound of time flowing between us became the sound of the water trickling quietly from the faucet until dawn.

Spring passed, and soon it was raining every day. A fine mist, like fluttering insect wings, dampened the trees and bushes that grew around the Light House. The days dragged by; the rain seemed always on the point of stopping but never did. I felt as though I was sleepwalking at school, waking only when I spotted Jun at the library or by the vending machines. As soon as classes ended, I headed for the sports center and the diving pool, and it was there alone, seated in the stands, that I felt myself come to life.

Life at the Light House was monotonous. After the rains set in, mold began to grow down in the kitchen and dining room: a lovely shade of green on a leftover roll and a snow-white variety on the apple pie one of the nurses had baked three days before. The sight of a garbage pail full of this decay aroused my cruel streak again, and I found myself imagining how Rie would scream if I sealed her inside. She would cry until she was covered with tears and sweat and snot; then a coating of mold, like colorful fuzz, would spread over her silky little thighs. Whenever I saw the pail, I imagined the mold on Rie's thighs.

One Sunday afternoon, I was in the playroom. Three of the youngest children, still too young for kindergarten, were playing together in a sea of toys. Rie was among them.

An early typhoon had passed to the west. The rain had stopped for the moment, and I was sitting near the window, listening to the wind.

A fight broke out over one of the toys, and Rie began to cry. I went over to pick her up. As she sobbed, she wriggled her fingers between the buttons on my blouse, searching for the comfort of a breast.

"You can't go outside to play," I told the other children. "The wind would blow you away." Then I took Rie to my room.

Reiko had gone to see her parents at the hospital and wouldn't be back for hours. Rie cheered up almost immediately and began to paw at the things Reiko had piled under her desk—cassette tapes for practicing English conversation, pennants she had collected on school trips, a flashlight with dead batteries. As I watched her, I wondered whether she had forgotten that I had shut her up in the urn and let her cry.

The wind shook the trees around the Light House. The roar seemed to wash over the building, amplified by the dense mass of leaves.

Under the desk, Rie was sorting through her discoveries, bringing each object to her mouth before moving on to the next. Her legs were stuck fast to the floor. Little children are like a different species, and I watched Rie the way another person might watch a rare specimen in a zoo. I wanted to pet her, to spoil her, but I didn't know how to do it.

I noticed a box wrapped in white paper that was peeking out of the open drawer of my desk. In it was a cream puff I had brought home four or five days earlier.

A fine rain had been falling on that day, too. The line of poplar trees around the sports center was veiled in mist. As I walked, I thought about the dives that Jun had been practicing and their degrees of difficulty. The soccer field and baseball diamond were deserted and silent, the only sound coming from the cars on the road beyond the trees.

A new pastry shop had just opened outside the center. The building was made entirely of glass, more like a greenhouse than a shop, and every detail of the kitchen—the knobs on the oven, the frosting bags, the knives and spatulas—was clearly visible. Large bouquets of flowers lined the doorway to celebrate the opening.

I'm not sure why I went in. I hadn't been particularly hungry. But the afternoon was dark and gray, and the rain hung over everything like a thick cloud of smoke. The shop, by contrast, was bright and cheerful, reminding me of the glittering diving pool; it was almost too bright. There were no other customers, and the display case was nearly empty. Like everything else in the shop, it was immaculate.

The cakes were like exquisite lacework. I bent over to examine them while a young woman in a frilly apron waited to take my order. I pointed at the last three cream puffs, lined up modestly in one corner of the case.

"I'd like those," I said.

The frilly young woman carefully transferred the cream puffs to a box, wrapped it in paper, affixed the shop seal, and then tied the whole thing with ribbon.

Carrying the cake box along with my schoolbag was somewhat difficult, and the safety of my new package obsessed me until I reached home. I ate one cream puff and gave one to Reiko, who, after thanking me with her usual exaggerated politeness, retreated to the top bunk to devour it. The third one I left in the box, which I put in the bottom drawer of the desk. Every time I opened the drawer, the white box seemed out of place, there among the ruler, the stapler, and a stack of photocopies; but I had almost forgotten about the cream puff inside.

I carefully removed the box from the drawer, as if I were handling something fragile. I expected it to be heavier, yet the box was as light as . . . a cream puff. I also expected to find a mass of brightly colored mold inside; however, the pastry looked almost as it had in the store—puffy and golden.

"Rie, come here. I have a treat for you."

She turned to look, and when she realized what was in the box, she came running happily to jump into my lap.

It wasn't until I cut the cream puff in half that I realized that the sweet smell of eggs and sugar and milk had been replaced by an acrid stench, like that of an unripe grapefruit. As Rie's lips sank into the cream, the smell filled the room. It nearly made me sick, but Rie devoured the pastry. Her eagerness was almost painfully sweet to see.

"Is it good?" I asked, but the wind drowned out the question.

I put the uneaten half of the cream puff back in the box and took it down to the garbage pail in the kitchen.

The wind continued to blow as the night wore on. The heat and humidity made sleep difficult. Every time I started to doze off, the sweltering air would drag me back from my dreams. Reiko had returned from visiting her parents, eaten a few pieces of chocolate, and gone to sleep without even brushing her teeth. As I listened to her sugary breathing, I could feel any chance of sleep slipping away.

I was about to check the clock to see how much time had passed when I suddenly heard footsteps in the hall. A door opened somewhere and then closed again, and I could hear anxious whispering. I kicked off my damp quilt and unfastened another button on my pajamas. Staring at the slats of the bed above me, I tried to make out what the voices were saying. I was wide awake now, my nerves jangling.

After a few minutes, I could distinguish my mother's voice over the rest. The others were muffled and subdued, but she sounded as agitated and sharp and somehow self-satisfied as ever. Even Reiko was roused from her deep sleep and leaned over to look down at me.

"What's happening?" she said.

I got out of bed, ignoring her question. My body felt strangely stiff, and I realized that I was exhausted from so many hours of trying to get to sleep. I opened the door and stood for a moment with my eyes closed, waiting to adjust to the light.

"Aya!" my mother called, pressing her hand to the front of her worn nightgown. "Rie's sick. She has a fever and terrible diarrhea, and she's been vomiting all night. Her lips are dry, and she has a strange rash. I don't know what's wrong with her. I wanted to call an ambulance, but your father said we should get that Dr. Nishizaki, the one with the clinic near the station. He says Nishizaki's a member of the church, so God will look after her. They're calling him now, but it's terrible, and in the middle of the night—all we can do is pray. Oh, Aya!"

The words came spilling out in one breath. The night nurse and the other employees who lived at the Light House stood around her, their faces drawn with fatigue and anxiety. There was something in my mother's tone hinting that she found the emergency almost thrilling.

I pressed my hands over my aching eyes, wondering why she insisted on chattering like that, why she had to explain everything when I already knew what had happened.

At that moment, Jun came up the stairs.

"I got through to Dr. Nishizaki. He said to bring her right away." He went into the children's dormitory and came out holding Rie. She lay like a limp rag in his arms. Her cheeks and hands and thighs were covered with pale pink spots, as if her body had rotted with the cream puff and was growing pink mold.

41

Jun carried her down the stairs, and everyone followed. My father was waiting in the car out front, the engine already running. Jun climbed in beside him, still cradling Rie.

Though I was responsible for her condition, I found myself watching Jun instead. He seemed so brisk and decisive, and his arms were muscular as they embraced Rie. His sincerity was almost more than I could bear.

Whenever there was an emergency—the time I fell in the river, the grease fire in the kitchen, or the earthquake that knocked over the china cabinet—Jun always managed to calm and reassure the rest of us. It was sad that someone could be so kind. The sound of the car engine faded into the night.

The others returned quietly to their rooms while my mother continued to call after the car. "Call me the minute you hear anything! I'll wait by the phone! If they send her to the hospital, let me know so I can get her things together!"

When they were gone, she turned to me, ready to launch a new soliloquy. "I hope it's nothing serious . . ." But I just nodded vaguely and said nothing, wanting to be alone with my thoughts of Jun.

I returned to the pool as soon as I could. It seemed all the more precious after I'd tasted deeply of my own cruelty. The ripples reflecting on the glass roof, the smell of the water, and above all the purity of Jun's glistening body—these things had the power to wash me clean. I wanted to be as pure as Jun, even if for only a moment.

In the end, Rie had gone on to the hospital. They said she vomited until there was nothing left and then slept for two days, as still and cold as a mummy. My mother went to the hospital to take care of her and came home with long reports. I wondered whether they'd found any trace of the cream puff.

I'm not sure how I would have felt if Rie had died, how I would have made sense of what I'd done. Because I had no idea where the cruelty came from, I could look at Jun's arms and chest and back without feeling the slightest remorse for having hurt Rie.

I was alone in the bleachers. It was as warm as ever. Voices and splashing hung like fog over the competition pool and the children's pool beyond it, while here there was nothing but the quiet splash of a diver entering the water, and then another.

Jun was wearing a navy blue suit with the insignia of our school embroidered at the waist, one of those we'd washed that night in the hall as we'd talked about the snowy morning. It was wet and clung to his hips. He had a habit of pulling at the wristbands he wore on each arm as he made his way to the end of the board. Then he would spend a long time getting the position of his feet exactly right.

"Back two-and-a-half in the pike position," I murmured.

It was a beautiful dive. His body was straight and perpendicular to the water at entry, and there was almost no splash. A few bubbles rose from the bottom, and then the surface was glassy again.

I liked pike dives better than tucked or twisting ones. When the body is bent at the hips and the legs and feet extended, the tension in the muscles is exquisite. I liked that shape of his body, with his forehead pressed lightly against his shins and his palms wrapped behind his knees.

As his legs traced a perfect circle in the air, like a compass falling through space, I could feel his body in mine, caressing me inside, closer and warmer and more peaceful than any real embrace. Though he had never held me in his arms, I was sure this feeling was true.

I let out a long breath and crossed my legs. The other members of the team took their turns diving, and between dives the coach shouted instructions through a megaphone. The swim team was practicing in the competition pool. A girl, apparently the team manager, was leaning out over one of the starting blocks and timing the laps with a stopwatch. Everyone except me was hard at work—but I, too, had a purpose in being here: to heal myself.

It wasn't until I'd passed the dressing rooms and the line of vending machines in the lobby that I realized it was raining. A hazy sun had been shining all day, so I was surprised by the sudden change; sheets of rain drenched the sports center, turning the poplars and the scoreboard and the soccer field dark gray. The enormous raindrops sent up miniature detonations as they hit the ground.

I stood helplessly by the door. It would take at least five minutes to get to the station, no matter how fast I ran; in rain like this I'd be soaked in five seconds. The prospect of riding home on a packed, rush-hour train in wet clothes seemed too depressing.

The couch in the lobby was already full of people waiting out the storm, while others were lined up at the pay phone to call for cabs. Seeing no alternative, I went outside. The air smelled of rain, of earth dissolved in rain. I sat down on the steps under the eaves and watched the drops pelting the ground. From time to time they splashed up on my socks.

Jun would still be at the team meeting or taking a shower, but I was worried that he would come out before it stopped raining. I had no idea how to face him if he found me sitting here. He would appear as he always did, fresh from his beloved practice; and I would be stained with the traces of Rie's tears and her rosy pink rash, which the pool had failed to wash away. I was about to run out into the rain when someone called my name.

"Aya!"

Jun's voice stopped me. I turned to find him standing above me on the steps. He looked fresh and clean, exactly as I'd imagined him, and for a moment I only watched him, unable to think anything to say.

"This is unbelievable," he said, his eyes moving from me to the rain.

"It is," I said. We stood on the steps, watching in silence. We had to stand close together to avoid getting wet, and through my skirt I could feel his gym bag rubbing against my leg.

I was grateful that he hadn't asked me why I was here, as if I had been forgiven some trespass. The rain was falling even harder, blotting out the world beyond the eaves.

"What happened to the rest of the team?" I asked. He was too close for me to turn to look at him.

"The coach gave them a ride home," he said, still gazing out at the rain.

"Why didn't you go with them?"

"Because I saw you leaving."

"Oh," I muttered. I wanted to apologize or thank him, but the words that came out of my mouth were the most dreary, practical ones: "Do you have an umbrella?" He shook his head.

"It wouldn't help much anyway," he said. "It's raining too hard. We should just stay here awhile."

Stay here awhile, I repeated slowly to myself, and with each repetition the meaning seemed to change, becoming "I want to stay here," then "I want to stay with you."

A taxi stopped in front of the building, its wipers beating frantically. A group of children who must have finished their swimming lessons came running out past us and dove into the cab, trailed by their mothers. But all the sounds—the hurried footsteps, the drone of the taxi's engine—were drowned out by the rain. The only noises that reached my ears were Jun's breathing and the thunder rumbling in the distance.

The raindrops continued to assault us, soaking Jun's shoulder; the fabric of his shirt clung to the curve of his back; but he seemed oblivious, listening for the thunder with childlike enthusiasm.

When I was with Jun, I often thought about our childhood: I recalled all the games we had played, just the two of us, in various places around the Light House. I had been alone with him when he drank the milk from the fig tree, and when we discovered the snowy hall. None of his school friends or his team-mates or the other children at the Light House shared these memories; I was the only one who had seen the expressions on his face at these moments, and I kept those images locked away like a bundle of precious letters. Then, from time to time, I would take them out to go over again.

Still, as time passed, the letters were becoming faded and brittle in my hands; and at some point, I stopped adding new ones to the bundle. Perhaps it was when Jun and I stopped being children—when the mere thought of him began to cause me pain, as it does still.

The thunder rumbled off into the distance; the rain, however, was as heavy as before. The damp spot on Jun's shoulder continued to spread, and I began to worry that he was getting cold.

"We should go inside," I said, tugging him by the elbow. He took one last look beyond the eaves and nodded.

We passed through the lobby and headed back to the pool. There was no one left in the diving well, but several men in swimsuits and T-shirts were collecting the kickboards and mopping the deck. The lights had been turned down; it seemed like a different place. Evening had arrived here even sooner than in the rainy world outside. We sat in the highest row of bleachers, our backs against the railing. The surface of the pool rippled gently below.

"This feels strange," I said, staring at his profile.

"Why is that?" he said, turning to look at me.

"I'm usually the only one up here in the stands. I sit here all alone and watch you on the board. But today, here you are, sitting right next to me."

"You always come to watch me practice, don't you?" His voice was so warm, so full of gratitude, that I could only nod.

Your body falling through space touches the deepest part of me. I murmured in my heart the words I could never say aloud.

"I come here straight from class and just sit and watch. I don't have anything else to do. I don't exercise, I don't do much of anything. I must seem like a useless old woman to you."

"You shouldn't be so hard on yourself," he said. "You'll find something that's right for you eventually. You just seem uncertain right now."

"Is that what you think?"

"It is," he said, nodding.

I wasn't at all sure whether I was uncertain or not, but he seemed so completely convinced that I let it drop. I suddenly felt quite peaceful, and I didn't know what to do next. My desires seemed simple and terribly complicated at the same time: to gaze at Jun's wet body and to make Rie cry. These were the only things that gave me comfort.

The mops scraped across the floor. The water level in the pool had fallen, as if a plug had been pulled, revealing a pattern of tiles in the wall.

"You never seem uncertain," I said, kicking my toe against the schoolbag I had left at my feet.

"There's no time for that when you're diving." He gripped the railing with both hands and raised his body, as if about to do a chin-up. "Maybe it's because there was something so uncertain and twisted about my birth, but when I'm up there on the board I just want to dive as straight and clean as possible, with no hesitation."

I was watching Jun's powerful fingers as they gripped the rail.

"Do you resent what your parents did to you?"

"No," he said, hesitating for a moment. "How can you resent someone you don't even know?" I suddenly felt terribly sad, as if I were only just learning that he was an orphan. No matter how kind he was to people, no matter how perfectly he performed his dives, he would always be an orphan. I wanted to breathe on his damp shoulder, to warm it with my breath.

The rain was beating on the glass above us. The pool was empty then, and the attendants had climbed in to scrub the bottom. The diving well was larger and deeper than I had imagined. They had turned off the lights above the bleachers, as if we were descending further into the night, and we were left in the dim glow that reached us from the pool.

We rambled from topic to topic—the extra math homework, our class trip, the school assembly—and occasionally we would look up at the rain. It seemed to be slowing.

"I wonder when Rie will get out of the hospital," Jun said at last, as if this were simply the next topic in our long, meandering talk. But the mention of her name pierced me like a thorn.

"I wonder," I said.

I pictured the scene in her hospital room from the one visit I'd paid her: the walls decorated with crayon drawings, the stuffed Mickey Mouse on her bed, and Rie herself stretched out lethargically on the wrinkled sheets.

"It was you, wasn't it?" His tone was so matter-of-fact, so unchanged, that I didn't understand immediately. "You did that to Rie, didn't you?"

The voice was the same, but this time the words began to sink in, as if they'd been replayed at a slower speed. There was no hint of blame or reproach in his voice, yet I felt a chill come over me.

"You knew?" My voice was hoarse.

"Yes."

"How?"

"I was always watching you." This could have been a breathless declaration of love or a final farewell. "I've known what you were doing to her for a while now." His eyes were fixed on the bottom of the pool. "Rie's had a hard time," he said, his voice low and even. "Her mother was mentally retarded, and she had Rie in a restroom."

If he had attacked me outright, I might have been able to defend myself. Instead, he exposed my secret as if offering himself to me. I was left mute, listening to my heart pounding in my chest.

I wanted him to stop talking. Anything he said would only make me sadder. Rie's sharp cries echoed in my ears, cutting Jun's shining muscles all to shreds. The world was spinning in front of me, as if I were falling head over heels into the empty diving well.

We sat for a moment, saying nothing. The railing had become warm against my back.

"We'll be locking up soon," one of the men called from the bottom of the pool. The spinning slowed.

"Okay!" Jun called back. "I hope the rain's stopped," he added, looking up at the ceiling. As I traced his profile with my eyes, I realized that I could never ask anything of him again: not caresses, not protection, not warmth. He would never dive into the pool inside me, clouded as it was with the little girl's tears. The waves of regret were gentle, but I knew they would ripple on forever.

"Let's go," he said, resting his hand on my shoulder.

"Where?" His palm was almost painfully warm.

"Home, to the Light House."

His voice reached me through the hand on my back. It struck me as a terrible joke that we were going home together, but I rose, nodding obediently.

PREGNANCY
DIARY

My sister went to the M Clinic today. Since she rarely goes to see anyone except Dr. Nikaido, she was nervous about the appointment. She had put it off, worrying about what she should wear and how she should speak to the doctor, until it was the last day they'd be seeing patients this year. This morning, she was still fussing.

"I wonder how many months of temperature charts I should show them?" She looked up distractedly from the breakfast table but made no move to get up.

"Why not take all of them?" I answered.

"But that's two years' worth," she said, her voice rising as she churned her spoon in the yogurt. "Twenty-four charts, and only a few days that have anything to do with the pregnancy. I think I'll just show them this month's."

"Then what was the point of taking your temperature every day for two years?"

"I can't stand the thought of some doctor pawing through them right there in front of me, as if he were trying to find out every detail of how I got pregnant." She studied the yogurt clinging to her spoon. It shimmered, viscous and white, as it dripped back into the container.

"You're making too big a deal out of it," I said, covering the yogurt and putting it back in the refrigerator. "They're just charts."

In the end, she decided to take all the charts, but it took her some time to find them.

I'm not sure why, when she was meticulous about taking her temperature, she was so careless with the charts themselves. The sheets of graph paper, which should have been kept in her bedroom, would stray to the magazine rack or the telephone stand, and I'd suddenly come across them as I was flipping through the newspaper or making a phone call. I realize now that there was something odd about my finding these scraps of paper with their jagged lines and telling myself, *She must have ovulated then,* or *Her basal temperature stayed low this month.*

My sister had chosen the M Clinic for sentimental reasons. I'd tried to get her to go somewhere bigger and better equipped, but she had made up her mind. "When we were kids, I decided that if I ever had a baby, I'd have it there," she said.

The M Clinic was a small, private maternity hospital that had been around since our grandfather's day. When my sister and I were girls, we had often sneaked into the garden to play. From the front, the three-story wooden building was gloomy, with moss-covered walls, a half-faded sign, and frosted windows. But if you made your way to the garden around the back, it was bright and sunny. For some reason, this contrast thrilled us.

There was a carefully tended lawn behind the building, and we loved to roll down it. As I rolled, glimpses of green grass and dazzling sky alternated in my vision, blurring to a pale turquoise. Then the sky and the wind and the earth would recede for a moment and I felt as if I were floating in space. I loved that moment.

But our favorite pastime was spying on what was happening inside the clinic. Climbing on stacks of empty boxes that had once held gauze or cotton balls, we'd stare through the window into the examination room.

"We'll get in trouble if they catch us," I said. I was always more timid than my sister.

"Don't worry, they won't do anything. We're just kids," she'd say, calmly rubbing the glass with her sleeve to wipe away the condensation from our breath. As we pressed our faces up against the window, we could smell the white paint inside. That odor, like an ache deep in my head, still reminds me of the clinic after all these years.

The room was always empty at midday, before the afternoon appointments began, and we could study it to our hearts' content. A collection of bottles arranged on an oval tray seemed particularly mysterious. They had no caps or seals, just glass stoppers, which I felt an irresistible urge to pull out. The bottles had been stained brown or purple or deep red by the fluids they held, and when the sunlight shone through them, the liquid seemed to glisten.

A stethoscope and some tongs and a blood-pressure cuff lay on the doctor's desk. The thin, twisting tube, dull silver fittings, and pear-shaped rubber bulb of the cuff made it look like a strange insect nestled among the other instruments. There was an odd beauty in the unintelligible letters printed on the medical charts. Next to the desk was a simple bed made up with faded sheets. A square pillow lay in the middle. It looked quite hard, and I wondered what it would be like to sleep on. A poster on the wall read "Position for use in treating breech presentation." In the picture, a woman in a leotard was curled up in a ball on the floor. She lay there in the yellowed poster, staring vacantly into the distance. Then the chimes from a school somewhere in the neighborhood would start ringing, telling us that it was time for the afternoon examinations. We knew that we had to leave when we heard the nurses coming back from lunch.

"Do you know what they do on the second and third floors?" I asked my sister one day.

"That's where they have the cafeteria and the rooms for the mothers and babies," she answered, as if she'd just been up to have a look.

Sometimes we could see women at the windows on the third floor. They had probably just given birth. They had on thick bathrobes, and their hair was pulled back in ponytails. None of them wore makeup. Wisps of hair floated around their temples, and their faces were expressionless. I wondered why they didn't seem happier at the prospect of sleeping above an examination room full of such fascinating objects.

My sister came back before noon, and I found her in the front hall just as I was getting ready to leave for work.

"What did they say?"

"I'm in the second month—exactly six weeks."

"Can they really tell that precisely?"

"They can when they have all the charts," she said, pulling off her coat and hurrying past me. She didn't seem particularly excited by the news. "What's for dinner?"

"Bouillabaisse," I said. "The clams and squid were cheap."

She had changed the subject so quickly that I completely forgot to congratulate her. But, then again, I wasn't quite sure congratulations were appropriate for a baby who would be born to my sister and her husband. I looked up "congratulate" in the dictionary: it said, "to wish someone joy."

"That doesn't mean much," I muttered, tracing my finger over a line of characters that held no promise of joy themselves.

DECEMBER 30 (TUESDAY), 6 WEEKS + 1 DAY

Since I was a little girl, I've disliked the thirtieth of December. I could always get through the thirty-first by telling myself that the year was finally over, but the thirtieth was confusing somehow, neither here nor there. Cooking the traditional New Year's dinner, cleaning the house, shopping—none of my tasks were completely finished.

When my father and mother got sick and died, one right after the other, my ties to the New Year's season became even more tenuous. Nor did things change when my brother-in-law came to live with us. Still, breakfast this morning was a bit more relaxed than usual, since I didn't have classes and my brother-in-law's office was closed for the holiday.

"When you haven't had enough sleep, even the winter sun seems too bright," he said, squinting behind his glasses as he lowered himself into a chair. The light shining in from the garden fell on the table, and our three pairs of slippers cast long shadows across the floor.

"Were you out late?" I asked. He'd gone to the year-end party for the dental office where he works, and I must have been asleep by the time he got home.

"I caught the last train," he said. As he picked up his cup, a sweet smell wafted across the table. He puts so much cream and sugar into his coffee that the kitchen smells like a bakery at breakfast. I've often wondered how someone who makes bridges and dentures for a living can drink such sweet coffee without worrying about cavities. "The last train is worse than the rush-hour ones," he added. "It's always packed, and everyone's drunk." My sister scraped her butter knife over her toast.

Since her visit to the gynecologist yesterday, her pregnancy is now official, but she doesn't seem any different. Usually the least little thing—her favorite hair salon closing, the neighbor's old cat dying, a water-main break—is enough to get her completely agitated and send her running to see Dr. Nikaido.

I wonder how she broke the news to her husband. I don't really know what they talk about when I'm not around. In fact, I don't really understand couples at all. They seem like some sort of inexplicable gaseous body to me—a shapeless, colorless, unintelligible thing, trapped in a laboratory beaker.

"There's too much pepper in this," my sister muttered, sticking her fork into her omelet. Since she always has something to say about the food, I pretended not to hear her. Half-cooked egg dripped from the end of her fork like yellow blood. My brother-in-law was eating slices of kiwi. I can't stand kiwi—all those seeds make me think of little black bugs, and the kiwi this morning was particularly ripe and soft. Beads of sweat had collected on the surface of the butter.

Apparently, neither of them was anxious to bring up the subject of the pregnancy, so I didn't mention it, either. Birds were singing in the garden. A few wisps of cloud dissolved somewhere far off in the sky. The clatter of dishes alternated with the sound of chewing.

None of us seems to have realized that the year is almost over. There are no pine branches decorating the door, no black beans or *mochi* in the house. "I suppose we should at least do the cleaning," I said, as if talking to myself.

"You shouldn't overdo it in your condition," my brother-in-law said, turning to my sister as he licked the kiwi juice from his lips. It's just like him to say the most obvious thing as if it were a profound truth.

JANUARY 3 (SATURDAY), 6 WEEKS + 5 DAYS

My brother-in-law's parents came to visit and brought a box of traditional New Year's foods. When they're here, I never know what to call them or what to talk about, and it makes me uncomfortable.

We had been hanging around the house all day with nothing more to eat than a frozen pizza or some potato salad, so the lavish display of holiday food was a bit overwhelming. It looked more like fine art than something you could eat.

I'm always struck by how nice they are. It doesn't seem to matter to them that the yard is buried in dead leaves or that there's nothing in the refrigerator but apple juice and cream cheese. They never have a bad word to say about my sister, and this time they seemed genuinely delighted with the pregnancy.

When they left in the evening, my sister let out a big sigh and collapsed on the couch. "I'm exhausted," she said and fell asleep as if someone had turned off a switch. She seems to sleep a lot these days; and she seems quite peaceful, as if she's wandered off into a deep, cold swamp.

I'm sure it has something to do with the pregnancy.

JANUARY 8 (THURSDAY), 7 WEEKS + 3 DAYS

Her morning sickness has started. I had no idea it came on so suddenly. She'd been saying all along that she wouldn't have it, that she hates that sort of cliché. She's convinced, for instance, that hypnosis or anesthesia would never work on her. But we were eating macaroni and cheese for lunch when she suddenly held up her spoon and began staring at it.

"Does this spoon look funny?" she asked. It seemed perfectly normal to me.

"It smells weird," she said, her nostrils flaring.

"Weird how?"

"I don't know . . . like sand. Did you ever fall over in the sandbox when you were little? Like that, dry and rough." She set the spoon back on her plate and wiped her mouth.

"Are you done?" I asked. She nodded and then rested her chin on her hands. The kettle began to whistle on the stove. She looked at me but said nothing, so I went on with my lunch.

"Doesn't the sauce on the macaroni remind you of digestive juices?" she murmured. I ignored her and took a sip of water. "So warm and slimy? The way it globs together?" She bent forward and peered at me, her head cocked to one side. I tapped the end of my spoon on my plate. "And the color, does it look like lard?"

I continued to ignore her. The sky was overcast, and a cold wind rattled the windows. The stainless steel counter was covered with the things I'd used to make the sauce—a measuring cup, the milk carton, a wooden spatula, and the saucepan.

"The noodles are strange, too," she added. "The way they squish when I bite into them makes me feel like I'm chewing on intestines, little, slippery tubes full of stomach juices." As I watched these words dribble out of her mouth, I fingered my spoon and thought how sad it was to see her like this. She went on talking until she had nothing else to say and then rose to go. The macaroni was a cold, white lump on her plate.

JANUARY 13 (TUESDAY), 8 WEEKS + 1 DAY

When my sister showed me the picture, I thought I was looking at freezing rain streaked against the night sky.

It was the size and shape of an ordinary photograph, with a white border and the name of the film company printed on the back. But when she got home from her exam and threw it on the table, I knew immediately that it was different from other photographs.

The night sky in the background was pure and black, so dark it made you dizzy if you stared at it too long. The rain drifted through the frame like a gentle mist, but right in the middle was a hollow area in the shape of a lima bean.

"This is my baby," my sister said, picking at the corner of the picture with a perfectly manicured fingernail. The morning sickness had made her cheeks pale and transparent.

I stared at the bean-shaped cavity. The baby was curled up in the corner, like a wispy shadow that might be blown away into the night by the first breeze.

"This is where the morning sickness comes from," she added, sinking heavily onto the sofa. She had eaten nothing since getting up this morning.

"How do they take these?" I asked.

"How should I know? I just lay there. As I was

getting ready to leave, the doctor handed it to me—as a 'souvenir,' he said."

"A souvenir?" I repeated, looking back at the picture. "So, what's he like," I continued, remembering the smell of the paint, "this doctor at M Clinic?"

"He's an older man, white-haired, quite a gentleman. He isn't very talkative, and neither are the two nurses who work with him. They don't say anything unless they have to. They're not so young themselves, probably about the same age as the doctor, and they look remarkably alike, almost as if they were twins. Their builds, their hair, voices, even the spots on their uniforms are in the same places—I can never tell them apart.

"It's quiet in the exam room, just a little shuffling of medical charts, tweezers clicking, needles being taken out of boxes. The nurses and the doctor seem to communicate by signals only they understand. The doctor just moves slightly or glances toward something and a nurse immediately hands him a thermometer, or the results of a blood test, or whatever. It's fascinating how they do it." She sat back on the sofa and crossed her legs.

"Has the clinic changed much?" I asked.

"Not a bit," she said, shaking her head. "After the elementary school gate, I turned at the flower shop, and when I saw the sign I felt as though I'd gone through a time warp. It was like being sucked back into the past." Her cheeks still looked cold and transparent from the walk.

"The examination room is exactly the same, too," she said. "That tall, narrow cabinet, the big chair where the doctor sat, the screen made out of frosted glass—it all looked just the way I remembered it. Everything seems old and out-of-date, but it's absolutely spotless. The only new addition is the ultrasound machine." She pronounced the words slowly, as if she were speaking about something very important. "Every time I go, they make me lie down on a bed next to it. Then I have to pull up my blouse and tug my underwear down below my belly. One of the nurses comes with a big tube and squeezes this clear gel all over it. I love how it feels, all smooth and slippery—it drives me crazy." She let out a long sigh before continuing. "Then the doctor rubs my belly with a thing that looks like a walkie-talkie; it's connected to the ultrasound by a black cable. The gel keeps it stuck to the skin, and they get a picture of what's inside on the screen."

Her finger reached out and flipped over the photograph that lay on the table.

"When they're finished, one of the nurses wipes my stomach with a piece of gauze. I always want it to go on a little longer, so that makes me a little sad." The words seemed to flow out of her. "When they're done, the first thing I do is go to the restroom and pull up my blouse again to look at my stomach. I always hope there's some gel left, but there never is. It's not even smooth when I rub it—I feel so let down." She sighed again.

One of the socks she'd pulled off tumbled to the floor. Outside, a light snow had begun to fall.

"How does it feel to have a picture taken of your insides?" I asked, staring out at the snowflakes dancing in the wind.

"I suppose it's about the same as when he takes an X-ray of my teeth."

"Your husband?"

"Yes. It's a little embarrassing, and it tickles." Her lips closed slowly, and she was quiet at last. She has a habit of talking for a long time without a break and then suddenly falling silent. But all that talking didn't seem to do her much good—she was always so nervous afterward. I was sure that she would be running off to see Dr. Nikaido before long.

The baby haunted the shadows that fell between us.

JANUARY 28 (WEDNESDAY), 10 WEEKS + 2 DAYS

Her morning sickness is getting worse. She seems convinced it will never get any better nor disappear, and that depresses her. At any rate, she can't eat anything. I've suggested just about every food imaginable, but she refuses everything. I even got out all the cookbooks in the house and went through them with her, but it didn't help. I realize now that eating is actually an extremely delicate undertaking.

Still, her stomach is so empty it must ache, and she finally said that she needed to put something in her mouth. (She couldn't bring herself to say "eat.") She decided on a croissant. A waffle or some potato chips might have done just as well, but a croissant left over from breakfast happened to be peeking out of the bread basket. She tore off a piece, forced it into her mouth, and swallowed it almost without chewing. Then, to wash it down, she took a tiny sip from a can of sports drink, grimacing with disgust as she swallowed. It didn't seem like eating at all, more like some difficult ritual.

My brother-in-law has been bringing home articles that he thinks will help: "How I Beat Morning Sickness" or "What Fathers Can Do for Morning Sickness." It's hard to believe, but the pregnancy seems to be affecting his appetite as well. At the table, he just pokes at his food and barely eats anything. "I can't eat when she's feeling so bad," he says, sighing. She seems to think that he's acting this way just to be nice, but I've noticed that when he's massaging her back while she forces down a croissant he gets terribly pale and clutches his other hand to his mouth. They huddle together like a pair of injured birds and shuffle off to their bedroom, not to be seen again until morning.

My brother-in-law seems particularly pitiful to me, since he has no reason to feel sick, and I find myself getting angry over his little sighs and whimpers. It occurs to me that I'd fall in love with a man who could put away a three-course French dinner even when he knew I was paralyzed by morning sickness.

FEBRUARY 6 (FRIDAY), 11 WEEKS + 4 DAYS

I eat all my meals alone now. I take my time, looking out at the flower beds or the shovel abandoned in the garden or the clouds floating by. I enjoy these quiet moments, and I sometimes even have a beer at lunch or smoke a cigarette, which my sister hates. I'm not lonely. Eating by myself seems to suit me. But this morning, as I was frying some bacon and eggs, she came running down the stairs.

"What's that awful smell?" she screamed, tearing at her hair. "Can't you *do* something?" She seemed ready to burst into tears. The bare feet protruding from the legs of her pajamas looked icy and as transparent as glass. She switched off the burner, nearly tearing the knob from the stove.

73

"It's just bacon and eggs," I whispered.

"Then why is the whole house filled with that disgusting smell? Butter, grease, egg, pork—I can't breathe!" Putting her head down on the table, she began to sob. I didn't know what to do, so I turned on the exhaust fan and opened a window.

By this time, she was crying in earnest. It was remarkable to watch, almost like a scene from a play. Her hair hung down over her face, and her shoulders heaved. I put my hand on her back to comfort her.

"You have to *do* something!" she said between sobs. "When I woke up, my whole body was filled with that awful stench. It's in my mouth and my lungs. My insides feel like they're coated with it. How did that awful smell take over the whole house?"

"I'm sorry," I said timidly. "I'll try to be more careful."

"It's not just the bacon and eggs. It's the frying pan and the dishes, the soap in the bathroom, the curtains in the bedroom—everything stinks. It's spreading all over the house, like a giant amoeba eating up all the other odors around it, on and on forever." She sat there weeping, her tear-covered face resting on the table, and I stood, my hand still on her back, studying the check pattern on her pajamas. The motor on the exhaust fan sounded louder than usual.

"Do you know how terrifying odors can be?" she

asked. "You can't get away from them. I want to go somewhere where nothing smells, like a sterile room in a hospital, where I could pull out my guts and wash them clean."

"I know, I know," I murmured. I took a deep breath, but I couldn't smell anything at all. Just the kitchen in the morning. The coffee cups were lined up neatly in the cupboard. The white dish towels were drying on the rack. A patch of frozen blue sky was visible through the window.

I have no idea how long she cried. It might have been only a few minutes, but it seemed much longer. In any case, she cried until she couldn't cry anymore. Then she let out a long, slow breath and looked up at me. Her cheeks and eyelashes were damp with tears, but her expression was calm.

"It's not that I don't want to eat," she said quietly. "In fact, I'm starved and I feel as though I could eat just about anything. I get sad when I remember how I used to enjoy it. I go back over old meals in my head—roses on the table, candles reflected in the wineglasses, steam rising from the soup or a roast. Of course, nothing has any smell in my imagination. But I think a lot about what I'll eat first when the morning sickness ends—if it ever ends. I try to picture it: sole meunière or spareribs or broccoli salad. I imagine every detail, so it's more real than real. I think about eating day and night—like a kid starving during the war. I guess that must sound silly."

She rubbed at her tears with the sleeve of her pajamas.

"Not at all," I said. "There's nothing you can do."

"Thank you," she muttered.

"From now on, I won't use the kitchen when you're here," I said. She nodded. My cold bacon and eggs lay quietly in the pan.

FEBRUARY 10 (TUESDAY), 12 WEEKS + 1 DAY

Twelve weeks—and the morning sickness is as bad as ever. It clings to her like a wet blouse. Which may be why she went to see Dr. Nikaido today. Her nerves and her hormones and her emotions seem all out of whack. As she always does before these visits, she spent a long time deciding what to wear. She lined up all her coats and skirts, her sweaters and her scarves on the bed and studied them carefully. She also spent a lot of time on her makeup. I worry that all this fuss will make my brother-in-law jealous. The morning sickness has made her hips narrower, her cheeks a little sunken, and her jaw more defined; she's even prettier than ever. You'd never guess that she was pregnant.

I met Dr. Nikaido once, when he brought her home during a typhoon. He's a middle-aged man with an unremarkable face, and he made no impression on me at all. In fact, afterward I couldn't recall a single feature— thick earlobes, for example, or strong fingers—nothing. He just stood quietly behind my sister, looking down at the ground. Perhaps because his shoulders and hair were wet from the rain, he seemed terribly sad. I don't really know what kind of therapy he practices, but my sister has mentioned psychological tests and medication of some sort. In any case, she's been going to him since she was in high school, more than ten years now without a break, but I can't see that she's got any better. Her emotional problems seem to come in waves, like seaweed tossed around in the ocean, and she's never found a safe, calm shore to rest on. Still, she told me she feels much better when she's at his office.

"It's like when they're shampooing your hair at the salon," she said. "The feeling that someone's taking care of you—it's wonderful." Her eyes narrowed with pleasure at the thought of him.

But it's hard for me to believe that Dr. Nikaido is a good psychiatrist. As he stood mutely in the doorway on the night of the typhoon, he looked more like a frightened patient than a doctor.

The sun had set and a golden moon had risen in the darkness, but she still hadn't come home. "She shouldn't be out in this cold," my brother-in-law muttered. When a taxi finally stopped at the gate, he hurried out to meet her. Her eyes glistened as she unwound her scarf, and she seemed much calmer than she was this morning. But no matter how often she goes to see Dr. Nikaido, her morning sickness is as bad as ever.

MARCH 1 (SUNDAY), 14 WEEKS + 6 DAYS

It suddenly occurred to me that I haven't been thinking about the baby. I suppose I should be wondering whether it's a boy or a girl, what they'll name it, what sorts of baby clothes to buy. I imagine people usually enjoy thinking about those kinds of things. But my sister and her husband never talk about the baby in front of me. They act as if there's no connection between the pregnancy and the fact that there's a baby in her belly. Which may explain why it has no concrete existence for me.

At the moment, I use the word "chromosome" to help me remember that there's actually a baby in there. "Chromosome" helps me give it some kind of form. I once saw a picture of chromosomes in a science magazine. They looked like pairs of butterfly cocoons lined up in a row. They were oblong, and just the right size and shape to pinch in your fingers. The pairs were all different: some were curved at the ends like a cane, others were perfectly straight and parallel, and others were backed up against each other like Siamese twins.

When I think about my sister's baby, I count off these twin cocoons in my head.

MARCH 14 (SATURDAY), 16 WEEKS + 5 DAYS

She hardly looks pregnant at all, even though she's entering her fifth month. For weeks now, she's consumed nothing but croissants and sports drinks, and she's losing a lot of weight. Except for her visits to the clinic and to Dr. Nikaido, she stays in bed all day, as if she were seriously ill.

About the only thing I can do for her is to avoid creating any kind of odor, so I've changed every bar of soap in the house to an unscented brand, and I took the paprika and thyme and sage from the spice rack and put them in a tin. I moved all the makeup that was in her room to mine, and, since she'd started complaining about the smell of the toothpaste, my brother-in-law went out and bought a Water Pik. Needless to say, I try not to cook when she's around. But, if I absolutely have to make something, I take the rice cooker or the microwave or the coffee grinder out to the garden and spread a mat on the ground.

It's peaceful eating outside by myself, looking up at the night sky. The evenings are warmer now that spring is almost here, and the air feels soft. My hands and feet pressed against the mat are dull and numb, but everything else—the crepe myrtle, the bricks lining the flower beds, the twinkling stars—is sharp and clear. Except for a dog barking in the distance, the evening is perfectly still.

I plug the rice cooker into the extension cord I've strung out from the kitchen, and within a few minutes a cloud of steam rises from the vent and vanishes into the darkness. A packet of instant stew warms in the microwave. From time to time, a light breeze blows, rustling the leaves and carrying away the vapor.

I eat more slowly when I'm in the garden. The cups and dishes set out on the mat are all at slightly different angles. As I serve myself the stew, being careful not to spill it, I feel as though I were playing house. A faint light is burning in my sister's window on the second floor. I think about her, curled up in bed, surrounded by all those odors, and then I open my mouth wide to take in the darkness with my bite of stew.

MARCH 22 (SUNDAY), 17 WEEKS + 6 DAYS

My brother-in-law's parents came to visit, and they brought along an odd-looking package wrapped in a scarf. Even after his mother unwrapped it, I had no idea what it was. It was just a long strip of white cloth about a foot wide. My brother-in-law unfolded it, and then we could see that it had a design of a dog printed at the edge. The dog's ears were standing up, and it looked alert and lively.

"Today is the Dog Day of the fifth month," said my sister. Her voice was weak and she couldn't hide her nausea, even in front of her husband's parents.

"I hope you don't mind, but these are supposed to bring good luck." As she spoke, her mother-in-law brought out a piece of bamboo, a ball of red cord, and a little silver bell, and lined them up in front of us. Finally, she produced a pamphlet from a shrine explaining how to use all these things to make a charm for a safe delivery.

"It even comes with instructions," I said, duly impressed.

"They sell it as a set at the shrine," she said, smiling cheerfully. As I watched my sister's slender fingers play over the pamphlet, I wondered whether the dye in the material or the mysterious piece of bamboo would give off odors. We passed the charms around, nodding solemnly and turning them over in our hands.

As soon as they were gone, my sister retreated to her room, forgetting about the gifts from the shrine. My brother-in-law wrapped them in the scarf, just as they'd come. The bell made a faint tinkling sound.

"Why is there a dog on the cloth?" I asked him.

"Dogs have lots of puppies without too much trouble. So they use them on these charms."

"Do animals know the difference between an easy birth and a hard one?"

"I imagine they do."

"Do you suppose puppies pop out like peas popping out of the pod?"

"You've got me." The dog on the scarf seemed to be watching us.

MARCH 31 (TUESDAY), 19 WEEKS + 1 DAY

I got up early today, since the supermarket I had to go to for my part-time job was quite far away. It was foggy, and my eyelashes were cold and damp by the time I reached the station.

The job suits me because my boss always sends me to a different supermarket in an unfamiliar part of town, and I never go to the same place twice. The supermarket is usually situated on a little plaza in front of a train station, with a pedestrian crossing, bicycle racks, and a bus terminal nearby. As I watch people come into the store, it makes me feel as though I'd gone away somewhere on a trip.

At the service entrance, I flash my ID card from the employment agency and the guard nods gruffly. It's depressing in the back, with boxes and wet sheets of plastic and bits of vegetable littering the floor. The fluorescent lights are dim. I wander through the store with the bag that holds my equipment, looking for the best place to set up. Today, I chose a spot between the meat counter and the frozen-food cases.

First, I made a stand by stacking some boxes from the storeroom. Then I covered it with a floral-print tablecloth and set out a plate. I put crackers on the plate, took my beater from the bag, and began whipping the cream.

The noise of the beater echoes through the empty store, and I always feel a little embarrassed. I concentrate on whipping the cream, ignoring the looks from the employees gathered around their registers for the morning meeting.

The store had just been renovated, so the floor was spotless and everything seemed to shine. I spooned little dabs of whipped cream onto the crackers and offered them to customers as they passed by. I always repeat the sales pitch exactly as it's printed in the manual from the agency. "Please try some. It's on sale today. What could be better with your favorite homemade cake?" I rarely say anything else.

All sorts of people passed by my stand—a lady in sandals, a young man in a sweat suit, a Filipino woman with frizzy hair. Some of them took a cracker from my plate and ate it. Some walked by with a skeptical look, and others put a carton of cream into their basket without saying anything. I gave them all the same smile. My salary has nothing to do with how many cartons I sell, so it seems easiest to be pleasant to everyone.

The first person to take a cracker today was an old woman with a bent back. She had what appeared to be a towel wrapped around her neck like a scarf, and a brown cloth purse in her hand. She was an ordinary old lady, almost invisible in the crowded supermarket.

"May I try one?" she said, coming up timidly to my table.

"Please do," I said, in my most cheerful voice.

She stared at the plate for a moment, as if she were examining some rare delicacy. Then she extended her dry, powdery fingers ever so slowly and took a cracker. The next motion, however, was amazingly quick. Her lips came open in a childish circle and she tossed the cracker into her mouth. As she bit down on it, her eyes closed appreciatively.

We stood there in the supermarket, surrounded by an infinite variety of food—behind her, stacks of meat in slices, cubes, or ground; behind me, frozen beans and piecrusts and dumplings. The tall shelves were packed tight from one wall to the other, and each shelf was overflowing with food: vegetables, dairy, sweets, spices—it seemed to go on forever. I felt dizzy just looking at it.

The shoppers passed by, baskets in hand, as if bobbing along on a stream of groceries. It occurred to me that almost everything in the store was edible, and this seemed a bit sinister. There was something disturbing about so many people converging on this one spot in search of food. And then I remembered my sister, and the way her sad eyes stared at a tiny morsel of croissant, how she seemed about to cry as she swallowed and the white crumbs scattered forlornly across the table.

As the old woman had opened her mouth to eat the cracker, I caught just a glimpse of her tongue. It was a brilliant red—in startling contrast to her pale, fragile body. Her throat was illuminated for just an instant, as the grainy surface caught the light. The whipped cream slid smoothly over her tongue and out of sight.

"Would you mind if I had another?" she said. As she bent over my plate, her purse swung back and forth in her hand. It was rare for anyone to ask for a second cracker, and I hesitated for a moment. But I caught myself almost immediately.

"Of course," I said, smiling back at her. She took another cracker in her wrinkled fingers and tossed it into her mouth, and again her crimson tongue peeked out from between her teeth. She seemed to have a healthy appetite, and there was a certain rhythm and energy to the way she ate.

"Thank you," she said, putting a container of cream in her basket.

"Thank you," I said, wondering what she would do with it when she got home. She turned, and a moment later she had disappeared into the crowd.

APRIL 16 (THURSDAY), 21 WEEKS + 3 DAYS

My sister put on a maternity dress for the first time to-day. Her belly suddenly seemed larger, but when she let me touch it, I could tell that it hadn't changed. I found it difficult to believe that there was a living be-ing there under my hand. She seemed to be having a hard time getting used to the dress and kept fiddling with the ribbon around her waist.

But her morning sickness has vanished, ending just as abruptly as it began. Since the nausea started, she'd avoided the kitchen completely, so I was puzzled when I found her leaning against the counter this morning, after saying good-bye to her husband.

Because we haven't been cooking, the kitchen was spotless. Every utensil had been put away, the counter was clean and dry, and the dishwasher was empty. It seemed cold and forbidding, like a showroom. She looked around for a moment and then sat down at the table. Normally, it would have been cluttered with bottles and containers we'd forgotten to put away, but today there was nothing on it. She looked up at me as if she had something to say. The hem of her dress swirled around her ankles.

"Would you like a croissant?" I said, trying to be as discreet as possible.

"Please don't even say that horrible word," she said. I nodded obediently. "But I would like to try something else," she continued, almost whispering.

"Sure," I said. I hurried to the refrigerator, realizing that this was the first time in weeks that she'd expressed any interest in food. But there was absolutely nothing there, just a bare lightbulb illuminating the emptiness. I closed the door with a sigh and went to look in the pantry, but there was nothing there, either.

"Don't you have anything?" she said, sounding worried.

"Let's see," I said, sorting through the bags and cans and jars. "There's a little gelatin, half a sack of flour, some dried mushrooms, red food coloring, yeast, vanilla extract . . ." I came across two leftover croissants, but I quickly put them back.

"But I want to eat something," she said, as if making a momentous decision.

"Hold on. There must be something around here." I checked the pantry again, shelf by shelf. At the very bottom, I found some raisins we'd once bought for a cake. The date on the box said that they were more than two years old, and they were as dried out as a mummy's eyeballs. "How about these?" I asked, pushing the bag toward her. She nodded.

It was strange to watch her eat something so hard with such a satisfied expression. Her jaw worked quickly as she took handful after handful from the bag. Her whole mind and body seemed to be concentrated on eating. When she came to the last few raisins, she let them rest on her palm for a moment, studying them lovingly before slowly putting them in her mouth. That was when I understood that her morning sickness was truly gone.

MAY 1 (FRIDAY), 23 WEEKS + 4 DAYS

In the past ten days my sister has gained back the ten pounds she lost during fourteen weeks of morning sickness. Now she seems to have something edible in her hand at every waking moment. If she's not at the table for a meal, she's clutching a bag of pastries, or looking for the can opener, or poking around in the refrigerator. It's as if her whole being had been swallowed up by her appetite.

She eats all the time, almost as a reflex, like breathing. Her eyes are clear and expressionless, fixed somewhere off in space. Her lips move vigorously, like the thighs of a sprinter. But for me very little has changed;

it's just like when she was sick all the time—all I can do is sit back and watch.

She suddenly has an appetite for all sorts of strange things. One rainy night she announced that she was dying for loquat sherbet. It was raining so hard that the yard seemed to be hidden behind a curtain of white spray, and it was very late. We were all in our pajamas. It seemed unlikely that any store in the neighborhood would be open, not to mention the fact that I wasn't even sure there was such a thing as loquat sherbet.

"I want loquat sherbet," she said. "Gold and icy, like the pulp of the fruit frozen into tiny crystals."

"I'm not sure we'll find it tonight," said my brother-in-law, as nicely as he could. "But I'll try in the morning."

"No. I want it now. My head feels like it's full of loquats—I'll never get to sleep unless I have it." Her tone was deadly serious. I sat down on the couch, my back to the two of them.

"Does it have to be loquat? They might have orange or lemon at the convenience store." My brother-in-law had found the car keys.

"Are you really going out in this rain?" I called to him, unable to hide my amazement.

"It has to be loquat," she said, ignoring me. "I can practically taste it . . . but it's not really for me. . . ."

Her husband put his arm around her shoulder. "Why don't you take one of those pills Dr. Nikaido gave you and try to get some sleep?" he said, fiddling distractedly with the keys. There was something irritating about the way he kept glancing at her as he spoke.

MAY 16 (SATURDAY), 25 WEEKS + 5 DAYS

Sometimes I think about my sister's relationship with her husband—particularly about his role in the pregnancy, if he ever had one.

When she's having one of her crises, he looks at her timidly and stammers meaningless little phrases meant to comfort her, but in the end all he can do is put his arm around her. Then he gets this sweet expression, as though he's sure that's all she really wanted anyway.

I knew that he was a bit dull the first time I met him. It was at the dentist's office. My sister had never brought him home while they were dating, or even after they got engaged; but when I got a cavity, she suggested I go to his office.

A talkative, middle-aged woman worked on my teeth, and when she found out I was related to the fiancée of one of their employees, she asked me all about my sister. At the end of every question, I had to close my mouth, which was full of saliva, and come up with an answer. It was exhausting.

When it came time to make a mold of my teeth for a crown, he appeared through a door at the back of the examination room. Since his job was to make bridge-work, he wore a white coat that was shorter than the ones worn by the dentists. He was a bit thinner back then, his hair a little longer. As he came up to me and muttered some standard greeting, I realized how nervous he was. His voice was muffled under his mask. Trapped as I was in the dentist's chair, I had no idea how to return the greeting, so I just turned my head toward him and nodded.

"If you'll allow me then," he said, with exaggerated politeness, bending down over me. The tooth in question was at the very back, so I had to open my mouth as wide as possible. He brought his face close to mine and stuck his hand in my mouth to feel around the root of the tooth. His fingers were damp and smelled of disinfectant. I could hear him breathing through the mask.

The dentist moved over to work on the patient in the next chair. Her cheerful voice rang out over the motor of the drill.

"Your teeth are a beautiful color," he murmured to me. I had no idea teeth came in different colors, but with his hand in my mouth, I couldn't ask what he meant. "And so straight," he added. "Your gums are healthy, too—firm and pink." I wasn't sure why he felt the need to give a running commentary on the state of my mouth; I certainly didn't need to have someone describe my teeth and gums in such detail.

My face was warm from the large light above my head. Needlelike drills and larger ones with diamond-shaped bits were lined up on the table next to me. A stream of water spilled into the silver gargling basin attached to the chair.

After the examination, he sat down on a stool and took a small glass plate from a cart. He sprinkled a mound of bright pink powder on the plate and poured a few drops of liquid on the powder. Then he mixed it vigorously with a tiny spatula. The string that held his mask swung back and forth behind his head, and his eyes darted restlessly between my mouth, my chart, and the glass plate.

As I watched the pink powder thicken, I wondered to myself whether this poor man, wrapped in his mask and his white jacket, was really going to marry my sister. "Marry" didn't seem to be quite right, so I tried other ways of putting it—"live with" or "love" or "sleep with my sister"—but none of these seemed right, either. He continued to grind away at the plate, apparently oblivious to the terrible noise that the spatula made against the glass.

At last the powder congealed into a malleable pink mass. He pinched it between his fingers and, using his other hand to hold open my mouth, smeared it over my molar. It was cold and tasteless against my tongue. As the tip of his finger ran over the inside of my mouth, I fought the urge to bite down with all my might.

MAY 28 (THURSDAY), 27 WEEKS + 3 DAYS

The more my sister eats, the more her belly grows. The swelling starts just below her breasts and continues down to her lower abdomen. When she let me touch it, I was surprised at how hard it was. And it isn't perfectly symmetrical; it lists slightly to one side. That, too, was something of a shock.

"This is about the time that the eyelids separate," she told me. "If the fetus is a boy, the genitals are starting to descend from the abdominal cavity." Her tone, as she described the baby, was cool. And there was something disturbing about the words she used— "fetus," "genitals," "abdominal cavity"—something that seemed inappropriate for an expectant mother. As I watched her belly, I wondered whether the chromosomes in there were normal, whether the cocoons were wriggling somewhere deep inside her.

There was a little accident at the supermarket where I was working today. One of the stock boys slipped on a piece of lettuce and broke a whole cart full of eggs. It happened right next to where I was doing my demonstration, so I saw it all at close range. There were broken eggs and slimy smears of yellow all over the floor. The tread mark from the boy's sneaker was still visible on the lettuce leaf. And several cartons landed in the fruit section, covering the apples and melons and bananas with dripping egg white.

After the accident, the manager gave me a big bag of grapefruits that he said he couldn't sell, and I was happy to take them home since there never seems to be enough food at our house these days. When I put them out on the table in the kitchen, I noticed that they still smelled slightly of egg. They were big yellow grape-fruits, imported from America, and I decided to make them into jam.

It was hard work peeling them all and getting the fruit out of the sections. My sister and her husband had gone out for Chinese food. Night was falling, and the house was silent except for the occasional tapping of the knife against the pot, a grapefruit rolling across the table, or my quiet cough. My fingers were sticky from the juice. The light in the kitchen illuminated the grainy pattern of the fruit. The grapefruits became even shinier when the sugar I had sprinkled on them dissolved. I dropped the pretty, crescent-shaped sec-tions into a pot, one after another.

The thick rinds strewn across the table were somehow comical. I cut the pith away and shredded the zest before dropping it into the pot. Yellow juice spurted everywhere, covering the knife, the cutting board, my hands. The zest, too, had a neat, regular pattern, like a human membrane seen under a microscope.

Finally, I turned on the stove and sat down to rest. The sound of simmering grapefruit drifted out into the night. Clouds of sour steam billowed from the pot. As I watched the fruit dissolve, I remembered a meeting that some fellow students had dragged me to a few months earlier. The title of the program was "Pollution: Our Earth, Our Bodies." There weren't many people there, but they seemed a sincere little group. As an outsider, I sat at a desk in the corner and stared out the window at a row of poplars lining the quadrangle.

A thin woman wearing old-fashioned glasses made a presentation about acid rain, and then there were several complicated questions. As I pretended to listen, I fidgeted with the pamphlet they had handed to me on the way in. On the first page, there was a picture of an American grapefruit with a caption in bold print: "Beware of imported fruit! Antifungal PWH is highly carcinogenic and has been shown to destroy human chromosomes!" The caption came back to me now in the kitchen.

The fruit and rind had dissolved into a smooth liquid

dotted with little, gelatinous lumps, and I had just turned off the stove when my sister and her husband came home. She came straight into the kitchen.

"What is that incredible smell?" she said, peering into the pot. "Grapefruit jam—how wonderful!" She had barely finished speaking before she had a spoon in her hand and was scooping up the hot jam.

"Not as wonderful as loquat sherbet," I muttered. She pretended not to hear, and, still clutching her handbag, in her new maternity dress and best earrings, she stuffed the spoon in her mouth. Her husband stood watching from the doorway.

She ate spoonful after spoonful. Her protruding belly made her look almost arrogant as she stood there by the stove, pouring the sticky globs of fruit down her throat. As I studied the last puddles of jam trembling slightly at the bottom of the pan, I wondered whether PWH would really destroy chromosomes.

JUNE 15 (MONDAY), 30 WEEKS + 0 DAYS

Monsoon season has started, and it's been raining almost every day. It's dark and gloomy, and we have to keep the lights on all the time. The sound of the rain echoes constantly in my ears, and it's so cold that I've started to wonder if summer will ever come.

But there has been no change in my sister's appetite,

and fat is beginning to accumulate in her cheeks and neck, her fingers and her ankles. Thick, soft fat.

I feel a little disoriented every time I see her like this. Her whole body is swelling before my eyes like a giant tumor.

And I'm still making my jam. Grapefruits are piled all over the kitchen—in the fruit basket, on the refrigerator, next to the spice rack. I peel them, dig out the fruit, sprinkle it with sugar, and simmer it gently over a low flame. Then, before I can get the jam into a bowl, she eats it. She sits at the table, cradling the pot in her arm and working her spoon. She doesn't bother to spread it on bread or anything else. From the motion of the spoon and the movement of her jaw, you'd think she was eating something hearty and nourishing, like curry and rice. It's a strange way to eat jam.

The acid odor of the fruit mixes with the smell of the rain. She hardly seems to notice me, but I sit there anyway and watch her eat. "Won't you upset your stomach if you eat too much?" I murmur. Or "Haven't you had enough?" Still no response. My voice is drowned out by the sound of the jam dissolving on her tongue or the drumming of the rain.

But I think the reason I watch her so closely has less to do with how she eats than with the strange way she looks. Her belly has grown so large that it's thrown all the other parts of her body out of balance—her calves and her cheeks, her palms and her earlobes, her thumbnails and her eyelids. As she slurps down the jam, the fat on her neck wriggles back and forth, and the handle of the spoon disappears into her swollen fingers. I take my time, examining every part of her, one after another.

Finally, when she has licked the last spoonful clean, she glances up at me with a sweet, dreamy look.

"Is there any more?" she murmurs.

"I'll make more tomorrow," I say, my voice flat and expressionless. And then, when I've cooked every last grapefruit in the house, I buy a new bag at the supermarket where I go to work. I always make sure to ask the man in the fruit department whether they're imported from America.

JULY 2 (THURSDAY), 32 WEEKS + 3 DAYS

It's almost the ninth month already. It seems as though the weeks have passed more quickly since the morning sickness ended. She spends nearly every waking hour eating now.

She came home from the M Clinic today looking a bit depressed. It seems that they warned her about gaining too much weight.

"I had no idea the birth canal could get fat," she said. "They said that women who put on too much weight can have difficult deliveries." She seemed irritated as she pulled out the notebook she'd been using to keep track of the pregnancy. I could see that someone had written "Weight restriction" in bright red letters on one page. "They told me that I should only gain about twenty-five pounds by the end of the pregnancy. No doubt about it, I'm in trouble." She ran her hand through her hair and sighed. She has already gained close to forty-five pounds.

"I don't suppose there's anything you can do about it," I muttered, glancing at her swollen fingers as I headed into the kitchen to make more jam. Because, without my really thinking about it, making grapefruit jam has become something of a habit. I make it and she eats it, as easily and naturally as you brush your hair when you get up in the morning. "Are you really afraid of having a difficult delivery?" I asked, without looking up from the counter.

"Of course," she said, her voice thin and faint. "These past few days I've been thinking a lot about pain— trying to imagine the worst pain I've ever felt, whether labor pains are more like terminal cancer or like having both legs amputated, that sort of thing. But it's pretty hard to visualize pain, and not much fun trying."

"I can imagine," I said, peeling fruit. She was clutching her notebook. The picture of a baby on the cover was warped, and the child seemed to be crying.

"But it's even more frightening to think about meeting the baby," she said. Her gaze dropped to her swollen belly. "I just can't believe that this thing in here is really my baby. It still seems so vague and abstract. But I know there's no way I can escape it. In the morning, when I'm just waking up, there's always a moment when I'm sure that it's all a dream—the morning sickness, the clinic, this belly, everything. It makes me feel wonderfully free. But then I look down at myself and I know it's real. I'm filled with sadness, and I realize that what scares me most is the thought of meeting my own baby."

I listened without turning to look at her. Lowering the heat on the stove, I stirred a big spoon through the pot. "It's nothing to be afraid of. A baby is just a baby. They're soft and cuddly, with little curled-up fingers, and they cry a lot. That's all." I stared down at the jam curling around the spoon.

"But it's not that simple. Once it's born, it's mine whether I want it or not. And there's nothing I can do about it, even if it has a birthmark covering half its face, or its fingers are stuck together, or it has no brain, or it's Siamese twins. . . ." She went on for some time listing awful possibilities. The spoon made a dull sound scraping the bottom of the pan as the jam began to congeal.

I stared into the pot, wondering how much PWH it contained. Under the fluorescent light, the jam reminded me of a chemical, something in a clear bottle, perfect for dissolving chromosomes.

"It's done," I said. Gripping the handles of the pot, I turned to face her. "Here, have some." I held it out to her, and she looked at it for a moment. Then, without another word, she started to eat.

JULY 22 (WEDNESDAY), 35 WEEKS + 2 DAYS

My summer vacation has started. I suppose it will be spent watching my sister's pregnancy. Still, a pregnancy doesn't last forever. It has to end sometime.

I've tried to think of the baby as something positive for my sister and her husband, and for me. But I never quite manage. I just can't imagine the look in my brother-in-law's eyes when he holds the baby in his arms, or the whiteness of my sister's breasts when she's nursing it. All I see is the photograph of chromosomes in the science magazine.

AUGUST 8 (SATURDAY), 37 WEEKS + 5 DAYS

So we've reached the month for her delivery, and she could go into labor any day now. Her belly is about as large as it can get, and I find myself worrying whether her organs can function properly when they're so compressed.

The three of us wait quietly, though the house is terribly hot and humid. We say nothing about it, but we're all thinking of the approaching delivery. My sister's shoulders heave as she tries to catch her breath. My brother-in-law waters the yard with the hose. The only sound is the humming of the fan as it turns on its stand.

I'm usually anxious when I'm waiting for something—even when it's someone else's labor pains. It scares me to think how nervous my sister must be. I'd like this hot, uneventful afternoon to go on forever.

But even in this heat, she is still lapping up my grapefruit jam as soon as it's done. She swallows it so quickly I'm afraid she'll burn her mouth, and I don't see how she can taste it at all. Her face looks sad, almost as if she were weeping, as I see it in profile, bent over the pot. The spoon flits back and forth from the pot to her mouth, and she seems to be trying to hold back the tears welling up in her eyes. This afternoon, the yard beyond her was glowing brilliant green in the sunlight. The cries of the cicadas were deafening.

"I can't wait to see the baby," I murmured. The spoon stopped for a moment and she blinked at me. But then she went back to the jam, and my thoughts returned to the shape of the damaged chromosomes.

AUGUST 11 (TUESDAY), 38 WEEKS + 1 DAY

When I got back from work there was a note from my brother-in-law on the table: "The contractions have started. We've gone to the clinic." I read these few words over and over. Out of the corner of my eye, I could see a spoon coated with jam lying on the table. I tossed it into the sink and thought about what I should do. Then I read the note one more time and left the house.

Everything was bathed in light. The windshields of the cars in the street seemed to glow, and the spray from the fountain in the park sparkled. I walked along, staring at the ground and mopping the sweat from my face. Two children in straw hats ran past. The gate to the elementary school was closed, and the playground was deserted. Farther on there was a small florist's, but I saw no sign of a salesperson or any customers. A tiny bunch of baby's breath lay in the glass case.

I turned the corner and found myself in front of the M Clinic. Just as my sister had said, time seemed to have stopped here, and the clinic was exactly as it had been preserved in my memory for all those years—the big camphor tree next to the gate, the frosted glass in the front door, the peeling letters on the sign. Here, too, there was no one in sight, only my shadow clearly etched on the street.

I followed the wall around to the back of the building and slipped through the old, broken gate into the garden. My heart started to pound the moment I set foot on the carefully tended grass, just as it always had. I looked up at the clinic, shielding my eyes from the glare of the sun reflected in the windows.

As I approached the building, the smell of paint drifted toward me. The air was still, and there was no sign of life around me. I was the only thing moving in the garden. I was tall enough now to look into the examination room without standing on a box, but there were no doctors or nurses to be seen. It was dark and deserted, like a science classroom after school gets out. I stood looking in at the bottles of medicine, the blood-pressure cuff, the breech-birth poster, the ultrasound monitor. The glass was warm against my face.

I thought I heard a baby crying in the distance. A tiny, trembling, tear-soaked cry coming from somewhere beyond the blaze of sunlight. As I listened, the sound seemed to be absorbed directly into my eardrums, and my head began to ache. I stepped back and looked up at the third floor. I saw a woman in a nightgown staring off into the distance. Her hair fell across her cheeks and her face was obscured in shadow, so I wasn't sure if it was my sister. Her lips were parted slightly, and she was blinking—the way you blink when you're close to tears. I would have gone on watching her, but the angle of the sun shifted and she disappeared into the reflection.

Following the baby's cries, I climbed the fire escape. The wooden stairs groaned under my feet. My body felt limp and warm, but the hand that gripped the railing and the ears absorbing the baby's cries were strangely cool. As the lawn receded slowly beneath me, its green became even more brilliant.

The baby continued to cry. When I opened the door on the third floor, I was blinded for a moment while my eyes adjusted to the light. I stood, concentrating on the baby's cry as it swept over me in waves, until at last I could see the corridor leading away into the darkness. I set off toward the nursery to meet my sister's ruined child.

DORMITORY

I became aware of the sound quite recently, though I can't say with certainty when it started. There is a place in my memory that is dim and obscure, and the sound seems to have been hiding just there. At some point I suddenly realized that I was hearing it. It materialized out of nowhere, like the speckled pattern of microbes on the agar in a petri dish.

It was audible only at certain moments, and not necessarily when I wanted to hear it. I heard it once as I was staring out at the lights of the city from the window of the last bus of the evening, and another time at the entrance to the old museum, as a melancholy young woman handed me a ticket without looking up. The sound came suddenly and unpredictably.

But the one thing all these moments had in common was that I was thinking, in each case, about a particular place from my past—and that place was my old college dormitory, a simple, three-story building of reinforced concrete. The cloudy glass in the windows, the yellowed curtains, and the cracks in the walls all hinted at its advanced age, and though it was meant to house students, there was no sign of student life—no motorbikes, tennis rackets, sneakers, or anything of the kind. It was, in short, the mere shell of a building.

Still, it wasn't exactly a ruin, either. I could feel traces of life even in the decaying concrete, a warm, rhythmic presence that seeped quietly into my skin.

But the fact that I could recall the place so vividly six years after moving out was due, no doubt, to the sudden reappearances of the sound. I would hear it for the briefest moment whenever my thoughts returned to the dormitory. The world in my head would become white, like a wide, snow-covered plain, and from somewhere high up in the sky, the faint vibration began.

To be honest, I'm not sure you could even call it a sound. It might be more accurate to say it was a quaking, a current, even a throb. But no matter how I strained to hear it, everything about the sound—its source, its tone, its timbre—remained vague. I never knew how to describe it. Still, from time to time, I attempted analogies: the icy murmur of a fountain in winter when a coin sinks to the bottom; the quaking of the fluid in the inner ear as you get off a merry-go-round; the sound of the night passing through the palm of your hand still gripping the phone after your lover hangs up . . . But I doubted these would help anyone understand.

A call came from my cousin on a cold, windy afternoon in early spring.

"Sorry to phone you out of the blue," he said. At first, I didn't recognize his voice. "It's been almost fifteen years, so there's no reason you should remember, but I'll never forget how nice you were to me when I was little." He seemed anxious to explain himself. "You used to play with me at New Year's and during summer vacation. . . ."

"It *has* been a long time!" I said, finally placing him. The call had caught me off guard.

"It really has," he said, letting out a sigh of relief. Then his tone became more formal. "I'm calling because I have a favor to ask." He got right to the point. Still, it wasn't immediately clear why a cousin, who was so much younger and had been out of touch for so long, should be calling to ask for something, nor could

I imagine what I could possibly do to help him. Instead of answering, I waited for him to continue. "You see, I'm coming to college in Tokyo in April."

"You can't be that old already!" I blurted out, honestly astonished. He'd been a boy of four the last time I'd seen him.

"And I'm looking for a place to live, but I'm not having much luck. Which is why I thought of you."

"Me?"

"Yes, I remembered hearing that you lived in a good dormitory when you were in school." My years in the dormitory came back as we spoke, but the memories seemed as distant as those of playing with this young cousin.

"But how did you know that I lived in a dormitory?"

"You know how it is with families—people talk about these kinds of things," he said.

It was true that it had been a good place to live. It was quiet and well run, but without lots of strict rules; and the fees were so low that it almost seemed the owner had no interest in making money. Unlike most places, it was privately run, rather than by a corporation or a cooperative, so it was technically a boardinghouse rather than what might normally be called a dormitory. But it was unmistakably a student dorm. The high-ceilinged entrance hall, the steam pipes lining the corridors, the little brick flower beds in the courtyard—everything about it said "dormitory."

"Yes," I said, "but it was a long way from the station, and the rooms were old and small even back then." I made a point of listing the drawbacks first.

"That wouldn't bother me," he said, as if he'd already made up his mind. "I just need something cheap." This was natural enough, since his father, my uncle, had died when he was still little—in fact, that was one of the reasons we'd been out of touch all this time.

"I understand," I said. "In that case, it might suit you."

"Really?" he said, sounding delighted.

"I'll give them a call. It was never very popular and there were always empty rooms. I doubt you'd have trouble getting in—if it hasn't gone under since then. At any rate, you're welcome to stay with us until you find a place—you can come whenever you like."

"Thank you," he said. I could tell that he was smiling on the other end of the line.

That was how I came to renew my ties with the dormitory. The first thing I had to do was call the Manager, but I had completely forgotten the number. I tried looking in the yellow pages. I wasn't sure a tiny place like that would even have a listing, but there it was, flowery advertising copy and all: "Heat and air-conditioning, security system, fitness center, soundproof music room. All rooms with private bath, phone, and ample closet space. A green oasis in the heart of the city." And the telephone number tucked in almost as an afterthought.

The Manager himself answered. He lived on the premises and served as both landlord and building superintendent, but to the residents he was always "the Manager."

"I graduated six years ago, but I was there for four years. . . ." He remembered me as soon as I mentioned my maiden name.

He sounded exactly as he always had. My memory of him was closely tied to his peculiar way of speaking, so there was something reassuring about hearing it again, completely unchanged after all these years. His voice was hoarse, and he seemed to be exhaling each word very slowly, as if he were doing deep-breathing exercises. It was an ephemeral sort of voice that seemed on the verge of being lost in the depths of those long, slow breaths.

"I'm calling because I have a cousin who'll be starting college this spring. He's looking for a place to live, and I was wondering whether you might have room."

"Is that so?" he stammered, sounding hesitant.

"Then you won't be able to take him?"

"No, I didn't say that," he muttered, but his voice trailed off again.

"Has the dormitory closed down?" I asked.

"No, we're still open. I have nowhere else to go, so as long as I'm around we'll be in business." There was something particularly emphatic in the way he said the word "business." "But things have changed since your time."

"What sorts of things?"

"Well, it's a bit difficult to explain, and I'm not quite sure I understand myself. But things are more *complicated* now, more *difficult,* you might say." As he coughed quietly at the other end of the line, I found myself wondering what sort of "complicated" or "difficult" circumstances a dormitory could fall into. "Actually," he continued, "we have very few residents now. I know there were some empty rooms in your day, but there are a lot more now. We can't serve meals anymore. Do you remember the cook who ran the dining hall?"

"Yes," I said, recalling the silent man who had labored away in the long, narrow kitchen.

"Well, I had to let him go. It was a shame, really— he was a fine cook. And we're only heating the large bath every other day. The deliverymen from the dry cleaner and the liquor store leave us off their route now, and we've given up all the dormitory events, even the cherry blossom picnic and the Christmas party." His voice seemed to be gradually fading away.

"That doesn't matter," I said. "That doesn't sound

so 'difficult' or 'complicated.' " Something made me want to try to cheer him up.

"You're right," he said. "The changes mean nothing in themselves. They're just an outer manifestation, the skull housing the brain, and what I really mean to say is hidden somewhere in the pineal gland, deep in the cerebellum at the heart of the brain." He spoke cautiously, as if weighing every word. An illustration of the human brain in my elementary school science book came back to me as I tried to imagine what sorts of difficulties the dorm was facing, but I was still drawing a blank. "I can't tell you any more than that," he said. "But in some peculiar way the dormitory seems to be disintegrating. Still, it's not the sort of thing that forces us to turn away people like your cousin. So tell him he's welcome, by all means. I'm so happy you remembered your old dormitory. Have him come around to see me, and ask him to bring a copy of his family registry and the letter of acceptance from his university—oh, and a copy of his guarantor's signature."

"I'll tell him," I said, and hung up, feeling a bit confused.

Spring was cloudy that year, as if the sky were covered with a sheet of cold, frosted glass. Everything—the seesaws in the park, the clock-shaped flower bed in front of the station, the bicycles in the garage—was sealed in a dull, leaden light, and the city seemed unable to throw off the last vestiges of winter.

My life, too, seemed to be drifting in circles, as if caught in the listless season. In the morning, I would lie in bed, looking for any excuse to avoid getting up. When I finally did, I would make a simple breakfast and then spend most of the day doing patchwork. It was the most basic kind of occupation: I would lay scraps of fabric out on the table and sew them together one by one. In the evening, I made an equally simple dinner and then watched television. I never went out to meet people and had no deadlines or projects of any sort. Formless days passed one after the other, as if swollen into an indistinguishable mass by the damp weather.

It was a period of reprieve from all the usual concerns of daily life. My husband was away in Sweden, working on the construction of an undersea oil pipeline, and I was waiting until he was sufficiently settled to have me join him. Thus, I found myself rattling around in the empty days, like a silkworm in a cocoon.

Sometimes I would get anxious wondering about Sweden. I knew nothing about the country—what the people looked like, what they ate, what sorts of TV shows they watched. When I thought about the prospect of moving to a place that was, for me, so completely abstract, I wanted this reprieve to go on for as long as possible.

On one of these spring nights, a storm blew through the city. It was louder and more furious than anything I'd ever heard, and at first I thought I was having a nightmare. Lightning flashed in the midnight blue sky, followed by enormous crashes of thunder, as if huge dishes were being smashed into a million pieces. A wave would roll across the city and explode right over the roof of our house, and before the echo had died away, the next one would come. It was so loud and close, I felt I could reach out and catch it in my hand.

The storm went on and on. The shadows around my bed were so dark and deep that they might have come from the bottom of the ocean. When I held my breath, I could see them trembling slightly, as if the darkness itself were quaking with fear. But somehow, even though I was alone, I wasn't afraid. In the middle of the storm, I felt quite calm—the sort of peace that comes from being far away from everyday life. The storm had carried me off to a distant place that I could never have reached on my own. I had no idea where it was, but I knew that it was peaceful. I lay in the darkness listening to the storm, trying to see this far-off place.

The next day, my cousin arrived.

"I'm glad you came," I said. But it had been so long since I'd talked with someone his age that I had no idea what else to say.

"I hope I'm not putting you out," he answered, bowing slowly.

He had grown a great deal since I'd seen him last, and I was quiet for a time, studying the young man standing before me. The relaxed lines of his neck and arms were brought together neatly around his muscular frame. But it was the way he smiled that made the greatest impression. He did it discreetly, his head slightly bowed, as the index finger of his left hand played over the silver frames of his glasses. A soft breath escaped between his fingers, and you might almost have imagined you'd heard a melancholy sigh. But there was no doubt that he had smiled. I found myself watching him closely to avoid missing the slightest change of expression.

The conversation proceeded fitfully. I asked about his mother. He gave me a quick update on his life from age four to the present. I told him why my husband was away. At first, there were painfully long silences between each new topic, and I would cough or mutter meaning-less pleasantries to fill them. But when we moved on to the topic of the times we'd spent together at our grand-mother's house when we were children, the conversation flowed more easily. My cousin had a surprisingly clear memory of that time. He had little sense of the context of the events, but he could clearly recall specific mo-ments in vivid detail.

"Do you remember how the river crabs used to come into the garden while we were sitting on the porch helping Grandmother clean string beans?" He seemed to be wandering back to a summer afternoon in the country.

"Of course," I said.

"Every time I found one, I'd yell for you to come catch it."

"I'll never forget the look you gave me when I told you that you could eat them. You'd never heard of catching something and eating it." He laughed out loud at this.

"When you put them in the pot to boil, they strug-gled for a while, trying to catch the edge with their pinchers, but then they'd get very still. Their shells turned bright orange. I loved to stand in the kitchen and watch them cook."

We went on for some time like this, comparing our versions of memorable moments, and each time I caught a glimpse of his remarkable smile, I felt myself opening up to him.

He had brought almost nothing with him to Tokyo, so we had to get the things he needed for the dorm. We made a shopping list on a sheet of notebook paper, numbering the items in order of importance. Then we discussed how to get as much as possible on his limited budget. We were forced to eliminate a number of things and try to make up for them in other ways. We gathered as much information as we could and then combed the city to find the best quality merchandise at the cheapest price. For example, a bicycle was at the top of his list, so we spent half a day going to five different shops to find a good, sturdy used bike. Then, we took an old bookshelf I had in storage and put a new coat of paint on it. I decided to buy his textbooks and some reference books as my gift to celebrate his entrance into the university.

The shopping took me back to my own student days, and it seemed to bring us closer together. As we gathered the items on the list, we felt the pleasure of accomplishing our task; and perhaps because it was such a modest goal to begin with, success left us with a sense of peace and contentment.

As a result of all this activity, I began to break out of my quiet cocoon existence. I made elaborate meals for my cousin and went with him on all his shopping trips. I even took him out to see the sights of Tokyo. The half-finished quilt lay balled up in the sewing basket, and a week passed in no time.

The day came for filing the official registration at the dormitory. It took an hour and a half and three transfers, but we finally arrived at the tiny station on the outskirts of the city. I hadn't been there since graduation, but it seemed that very little had changed in six years. The road outside the ticket gate sloped gradually up the hill. A young policeman stood in the door of the police box, while high school students on bicycles threaded their way through the shoppers in the arcade. In other words, it was much the same as every other sleepy Tokyo suburb.

"What's the Manager like?" my cousin asked as the noise of the station died away and we entered streets lined with houses.

"I'm not sure I know myself," I answered truthfully. "He's something of a mystery. He runs the dormitory, but I don't know exactly what that involves. It's hard to believe he makes any money from it, but at the same time it doesn't seem to be a front for a religious group or anything like that. It's on a fairly large piece of land, so it's a bit odd they haven't torn it down and built something more lucrative."

"It's lucky for me they haven't," my cousin said. "Maybe he runs it as a kind of public service."

"Could be," I said.

Twin girls, about elementary school age, played badminton at the side of the road. They were absolutely identical and were quite good at their game. The shuttlecock went back and forth in perfectly symmetrical arcs. A woman on the balcony of an apartment building was airing out a child's futon, and the faint *ping* of an aluminum bat came from the baseball diamond at the technical high school. All in all, an ordinary spring afternoon.

"The Manager lives in the dorm. His room is no bigger than the student rooms and not much more luxurious. He lives alone, and it seems he has no family. I never saw pictures of relatives, and I don't remember anyone ever coming to visit."

"About how old is he?" my cousin asked, and I suddenly realized that I'd never given any thought to the question. I tried to recall the Manager's face, but I had only the vague impression of a man who was no longer young. This was perhaps because he had cut himself off from so many things in life: from family and social status—perhaps even from something as mundane as age itself. He'd had no connection to anyone and had not seemed to belong anywhere.

"I suppose he's middle-aged," I said, for want of a

better answer. "But I don't really know much about him. Even when you're living there, you won't see him very often. Maybe when you go to pay your rent, or report a burned-out lightbulb or a broken washing machine. Not often. But don't worry, he's nice enough."

"I'm sure he is," my cousin said.

Spring had arrived suddenly after the night of the storm. The clouds remained, but warmth in the air seemed to announce the change of seasons. My cousin clasped the envelope that held his registration materials firmly under his arm. Somewhere in the distance, a bird was singing.

"There's one thing I forgot to mention," I said, finally bringing up the subject that had been on my mind all day. My cousin turned to look at me, waiting expectantly for me to continue. "The Manager is missing one leg and both arms." There was a short silence.

"One leg and both arms," he repeated at last.

"His left leg, to be precise."

"What happened to him?"

"I'm not sure. An accident, I suppose. There were rumors—that he'd been caught in some machine or was in a car wreck. No one could ever manage to ask him, but it must have been something awful."

"That's for sure," my cousin said, looking down as he kicked a pebble.

"But he can do everything for himself—cook, get

dressed, get around. He can use a can opener, a sewing machine, anything, so you won't even notice after a while. When you've been around him, it somehow doesn't seem to be very important. I just didn't want you to be shocked when you meet him."

"I see what you mean," my cousin said, kicking another pebble.

We made several turns and then crossed the street and began climbing a hill. We passed a beauty salon with old-fashioned wigs lined up in the window, a large house with a hand-lettered sign offering violin lessons, and a field of garden plots rented out by the city. These smelled wonderfully like soil. Everything seemed familiar to me, and yet it seemed almost miraculous that I should be walking here in this place from my past with this cousin whom I'd thought I would never see again. The memories of him as a small boy and memories from my days at the dormitory seemed to bleed together like the shades in a watercolor painting.

"I wonder what it's like living alone," my cousin said, as if talking to himself.

"Are you worried?" I asked.

"Not at all," he said, shaking his head. "Just a bit nervous perhaps, the way I always am when something changes. I had the same feeling when my father died, or when a girl I liked moved to a different school—even when the chicken I was raising was eaten by a stray cat."

"Well, I suppose living alone does feel a bit like losing something." I looked up at him. His profile was framed by the clouds as he stared off into the distance. It occurred to me that he was young to have lost so many important things: his chicken, his girl, his father. "Still, being alone doesn't mean you have to be miserable. In that sense it's different from losing something. You've still got yourself, even if you lose everything else. You've got to have faith in yourself and not get down just because you're on your own."

"I think I see what you mean," he said.

"So there's nothing to be nervous about," I said, patting him lightly on the back. He pushed at his glasses and gave me one of his smiles.

We walked on, talking from time to time and then falling silent. There was something else on my mind besides the Manager's physical condition. I kept thinking about what he'd said about the dormitory "disintegrating" in some "peculiar way," but I couldn't come up with a good way to mention this to my cousin. While I was still thinking, we turned the last corner and found ourselves in front of the dormitory.

It had clearly aged. There was no striking change in the overall appearance, but each individual detail—the doorknob in the front hall, the rails on the fire escape, the antenna on the roof—seemed older. It was probably just normal wear and tear, given how long I'd been away. But at the same time there was something deep and weary about the silence that hung over the place, something almost sinister that could not be explained away by the fact that it was spring break and the residents would be absent.

I paused for a moment at the gate, overcome more by this silence than by nostalgia. Weeds had grown up in the courtyard, and someone had left a helmet by the bicycle rack. When the wind blew, the grass seemed to whisper.

I looked from window to window, searching for any sign of life. They were all tightly closed, as if rusted shut, except one that stood open just a crack to reveal a bit of faded curtain. The dusty porch was littered with clothespins and empty beer cans. Still staring up at the building, I took a step forward and brushed lightly against my cousin. We looked at each other for a moment and then walked through the door.

Inside, everything was strangely unchanged. The pattern on the doormat, the old-fashioned telephone that took only ten-yen coins, the broken hinges on the shoe cupboard—it was all just as it had been when I'd lived here, except that the profound stillness made all these details seem somehow more solitary and forlorn. There were no students to be seen, and as we penetrated deeper into the building, the silence seemed to grow denser. Our footsteps were the only sound, and they were quickly muffled by the low plaster ceiling.

We had to pass through the dining hall to reach the Manager's room. As the Manager had said on the phone, it had been out of service since the cook had been let go, and everything was spotless and tidy. We made our way cautiously among the empty tables.

My cousin knocked on the Manager's door, and after a moment it opened haltingly, as if it were caught on something. His door had always opened this way, since the Manager had to bend over double to turn the knob between his chin and collarbone and then drag the door back with his torso.

"Welcome."

"Pleased to meet you."

"I'm sorry I've been so out of touch."

We muttered our respective greetings and bowed. The Manager wore a dark blue kimono, just as he always had. He had a prosthetic leg, but the sleeves hung empty at his sides. As he twisted his shoulder in the direction of the couch and told us to sit down, they flapped loosely against his body.

When I lived in the dormitory, I had always conducted my business with the Manager while standing in the doorway, so this was the first time I'd been in this room. I looked around with a certain curiosity. It

was a small but well-organized space, and everything in it had been designed to make his life easier.
Everything—the pens, the pencils, the dishes, the
television—seemed to have been carefully arranged so
that he would be able to manipulate it with his chin,
his collarbone, or his leg. As a result, the room was
completely bare above a certain height, except for a
spot in the corner of the ceiling about six inches in di-
ameter.

It took only a few minutes to complete the necessary
paperwork. There was apparently nothing preventing
my cousin from moving in, nor did the Manager mention the "peculiar disintegration" of the dormitory. After listening to the usual speech about the rules and
regulations, my cousin signed the contract in his neat,
angular handwriting. The contract was no more than a
simple promise to obey the rules of the dormitory and
live a "happy student life." As I watched him sign, I
whispered the word "happy" to myself. It seemed too
sentimental for a contract, and I wondered whether I
had signed the same document when I lived here. I certainly didn't remember it. In fact, nothing about the
scene seemed familiar, and I wondered how much I had
forgotten about the dormitory.

"Well then, would you like some tea?" said the
Manager. His voice was slightly hoarse, as it had always been. My cousin gave me a nervous glance, as if

he wasn't sure how to respond, and I realized that it was difficult to imagine the Manager making tea. But I gave him a look that was intended to say, "Don't worry, he can do almost anything." My cousin turned to face the Manager again, but his lips were still fixed in an anxious smile.

The tea canister, teapot, thermos bottle, and cups were laid out in precise order. The Manager braced himself on his artificial leg and swung his right leg lightly up on the table. It happened in an instant, almost too quickly for the eye to see, but there it lay, like a tree felled in the forest. There was an odd contradiction between Manager's awkward posture now, bent over the table, and the deft movement that had got him into this position.

Next, he took the tea canister between his chin and collarbone and twisted it open, just as he had done with the doorknob. Lifting the canister, he poured the tea into the pot. This movement was exquisitely graceful. The degree of force applied, the angle of the canister, the quantity of tea—it was all perfect. The supple line of his jaw and the fixed plane of his collarbone functioned together like a precisely calibrated instrument that seemed to become a separate living thing as we watched.

The pale light from the courtyard filtered through the window. Tulips were blooming in the flower bed. A single orange petal had fallen on the dark earth. Everything was absolutely still except the Manager's jaw.

My cousin and I watched his preparations as if we were attending some solemn ritual. Pressing the button on the thermos with his toe, he filled the teapot with boiling water, and then, still using his toes, he grasped the pot and poured the tea into the cups. The sound of the thin trickle of hot tea fell into the silence of the room.

The Manager's foot was beautiful. Though he must have used it much more than one normally would, it was flawless, without a single cut or bruise. I studied the fleshy instep, the sole that looked so warm and alive, the translucent nails, the long toes—and I realized I had never considered a foot so closely or carefully, not even my own, which I could only vaguely recall.

I wondered what sort of hands the Manager would have had, and I found myself imagining ten strong fingers extending from broad, fleshy palms, fingers that would have been as graceful and precise as his toes. My eyes wandered to the empty spaces at the ends of his sleeves.

When he had finished preparing the tea, the Manager coughed quietly and removed his leg from the table.

"Please, help yourself," he said, looking down almost

bashfully. We bowed and took our tea. My cousin held his cup in both hands and drained it slowly, almost as if he were saying a prayer.

When we had finished, we went to have a look at the room where my cousin would be living and then told the Manager we had to be going. He saw us to the door.

"We'll see you again soon," he said.

"I think I'll be very happy here," my cousin responded. As the Manager bowed, his leg squeaked unpleasantly, and the sound hung between us like a plaintive murmur.

Soon afterward, my cousin moved into the dormitory. It wasn't a complicated process, since he had very little besides the few items we had gathered. We packed these into a cardboard box and sent them by express delivery. Dismayed at the thought of returning to my cocoon existence, I puttered about in search of ways to delay his departure, even by a few minutes.

"I suppose college classes are completely different from high school," he said. "I'm worried I won't be able to keep up. Do you think you could help me with German?"

"Sorry, I took Russian."

"Too bad," he said. Despite his claim to be worried,

he seemed quite cheerful as he packed. No doubt it was the prospect of the freedom that lay ahead.

"Let me know right away if you have any trouble. If you run out of money, or get sick, or get lost . . ."

"Lost?"

"Just for instance," I said. "And come to dinner now and then. I'll cook something you like and give you advice about your love life. I'm particularly good in that department." He smiled happily as he nodded to each of my requests.

Then he headed off once more for the dormitory, this time by himself. I can't say why, but this simple parting affected me more than I would have imagined. I watched him walking away, sweater over his shoulders, bag in hand, until he was no more than a tiny point in the distance. I watched, without so much as blinking, and I realized how utterly lonely I was. But all my staring couldn't prevent that distant point from vanishing like a snowflake dissolving in the sunlight.

After he left, I returned to my usual routine: long naps, simple meals, and my patchwork. I found the half-finished quilt in the sewing basket and ironed out the wrinkles. I added patch after patch in every color and pattern, lavender and yellow, gingham check and paisley. First I pinned the seams, and then I would carefully sew the piece to the quilt. I became so absorbed in simply adding one patch to the next that I sometimes forgot what I was making. Then I would spread out the pattern and remind myself that I was working on a quilt or a wall hanging or whatever— before returning to the patches.

I looked at my hand holding the needle, and I thought of the Manager's beautiful foot. I thought of the phantom hands that had disappeared to some unknown place, the tulips in the flower bed, the spot on the ceiling, the frames of my cousin's glasses. They had somehow been wedded in my mind—the Manager, the dormitory, and my cousin.

Soon after school started, I went to visit. It was a beautiful day, and the petals of the cherry blossoms had begun to fall like tiny butterflies settling to earth. Unfortunately, my cousin was still at the university, but I decided to look in on the Manager while I waited for him. We sat on the porch and ate the strawberry shortcake that I'd brought for my cousin.

Though the new semester had started, the dormitory was as quiet as ever. At one point I thought I heard footsteps from deep within the building, but the sound died away almost immediately. When I had lived here, there was always a radio playing somewhere, or laughter or a motorbike engine racing, but now it seemed that all signs of life had faded. The orange tulips in the flower bed had been replaced by deep red ones, and a honeybee flew in and out of the crimson petal cups.

"Is he getting along all right?" I asked, looking down at the shortcake.

"Yes, he seems fine," the Manager said. "He ties his books on the back of his bike every morning and rushes off to school." Grasping the fork with his toes, he scooped up a bite of cake and whipped cream.

The tiny dessert fork suited his foot. The curve of the ankle, the delicate movement of the toes, the luster of the nails—it all went perfectly with the glistening silver.

"He says he's playing team handball. He must be quite good."

"I don't think so," I said. "He played in high school, but his team was only second or third in the prefecture championships."

"But he certainly has the build to be an athlete. You don't see too many people with bodies like that," the Manager said. "I should know." The bite of cake that had been trembling on his fork was deposited in his mouth, and he chewed it with infinite care. "When I meet someone for the first time, I pay no attention to his looks or personality; the only thing that interests me is the body as a physical specimen." As he spoke, he scooped up another bite of cake. "I notice little ir-regularities right away: an imbalance between the bi-ceps, signs of an old sprain in the ring finger, an oddly formed ankle. I catch those kinds of things in the first few seconds. When I remember someone, I think of the sum of the parts—the hands and feet, the neck, the shoulders and the chest, the hips, the muscles, the bones. There's no face involved. I'm particularly inter-ested in the bodies of young people—given my line of work. But don't misunderstand me—I'm not inter-ested in *doing* anything to them; to me, it's like look-ing at pictures in a medical dictionary. But I suppose that sounds strange."

I stared at my fork, unable to respond. The Man-ager swallowed the second bite of cake.

"I don't know how it feels to use four limbs. I sup-pose that's why I'm so fascinated by other people's bodies." I glanced at his artificial leg hanging over the edge of the porch. The dull metallic color peeked out between his sock and the hem of his kimono. He seemed to be enjoying his cake; after each bite he would lap the cream from the end of his fork and then carefully lick his lips.

"At any rate, I can assure you he has a marvelous body—perfect for team handball. Strong fingers to grip the ball, a flexible spine for the jump shot, long arms for blocking, powerful shoulders for the long pass . . ."

It seemed he could go on forever about my cousin's body. I listened uncomfortably as he formed his lips, still sticky from the whipped cream, around the words "spine" and "shoulders."

A soft breeze was blowing and the garden was filled with sunlight. The bee that had been hovering around the tulips flew between us and disappeared into the Manager's room, coming to rest in the middle of the spot on the ceiling. The spot seemed to have grown a good deal since I'd first seen it. It was still round, but the color had darkened, as if all the shades in the paint box had been mixed together. The transparent wings of the bee flashed brilliantly against the dark stain.

The Manager had been saving the strawberry on the top of his cake, but now he popped it in his mouth. There was still no sign of my cousin. I listened for his bike but heard only the droning of the bee's wings. The Manager began to cough quietly, as if he were muttering to himself.

In the end, I never saw my cousin that day. He phoned to say that he had something to do at the university and would be late getting home.

About ten days later, I paid my next visit to the dormitory. This time I decided to take an apple pie, but again I was unable to deliver the gift to my cousin.

"He just called to say that there was an accident on the train line and he was stuck somewhere." The Manager was out sweeping the yard with a bamboo broom.

"What kind of accident?"

"He said that someone jumped in front of the train."

"Oh," I said, clutching the pastry box to my chest. I pictured the body on the tracks, crushed like an overripe tomato, the hair tangled in the gravel, bits of bone scattered over the railroad ties.

Springtime had come to the dormitory. A gentle breeze softened even the broken bicycle abandoned in one corner of the garden. There was still a trace of warmth coming from the pie in the box.

"But you've come all this way," said the Manager. "You might as well stay awhile."

"Thank you," I said.

The garden was well tended, but the Manager worked the broom vigorously, sweeping the same spot again and again until he had gathered every leaf and twig. Bent over to hold the broom under his chin, he seemed lost in thought as he worked.

The bamboo scraped quietly in the dirt. I glanced up at my cousin's room and noticed a pair of tennis shoes hanging on the balcony.

"It's quiet around here," I said.

"It certainly is," the Manager agreed. The sound of the broom continued.

"How many students do you have now?"

"Very few," he said, a bit evasively.

"Other than my cousin, how many new students moved in this year?"

"He was the only one."

"But it must be lonely with so many empty rooms. I remember one time I didn't go home for the New Year's holiday, and I was so frightened I couldn't sleep." The Manager said nothing. "Are you advertising?" Still nothing. A deliveryman on a motorbike passed by outside the gate.

Suddenly, the Manager spoke up. "It's because of the rumor."

"The rumor?" I repeated, taken aback.

"It's the rumor that's keeping them away," he said, beginning his explanation as if he were telling a favorite story. "In February, one of the students suddenly disappeared. 'Disappeared' is the only way to describe it—it was as if he dissolved into thin air without so much as a whimper. I wouldn't have believed that a human being with a brain, a heart, with arms and legs and the power of speech could have simply vanished like that. There was nothing about him that suggested he would disappear. He was a freshman, studying mathematics. A brilliant student who had received a prestigious scholarship. He was popular, and he went out with his girlfriend from time to time. His father teaches at a university somewhere, and his mother writes children's books. There was a cute little sister, too. He seemed to have everything going for him. So it didn't make sense that he would suddenly vanish."

"There were no clues at all? A call, a note?"

The Manager shook his head.

"The police did a thorough investigation. They seemed to think he'd got himself mixed up in some sort of bad business, but there was no real evidence. When he disappeared, the only things he had with him were a mathematics text and a notebook."

The broom that had been propped on his shoulder fell to the ground, but he ignored it and went on with his story.

"The police called me in for questioning. . . . I was apparently a suspect. They wanted to know everything I'd done during the week he disappeared. Every word of the conversations I'd had with him, what books I'd read and what they were about, who had called me and what they wanted, what I'd eaten, how often I'd been to the bathroom—everything. They took down every word, recopied it, edited it, read it back to me. It was like sifting through every grain of sand on the beach. It took them three weeks to go over one week of my life—but in the end it was all a waste of time. And I was completely exhausted. The stump on my leg got infected and hurt like the devil. But they never found him."

"But I don't understand," I said. "Had you done something to him? Why did they suspect you?"

"I don't know. But the residents and the neighbors knew that I'd been questioned, and that was enough. They didn't say anything to my face, but the rumors must have been cruel. And since then almost everyone has moved out."

"How awful!"

"Rumors have a life of their own. But what bothers me more is that enormous file they made on my private life. I have no idea where it ended up, and that gives me a sick feeling."

He closed his eyes and started coughing. He tried to say something, apologize perhaps, but ended up coughing even harder. Finally, he was bent double and gasping.

"Are you all right?" I asked, resting my hand on his back. As I did so, I realized that it was the first time I had ever touched him. The material of his kimono was coarse and thick, but the body under it was so fragile I was afraid it might break from the weight of my hand. The vibrations ran through me as he continued to cough. "You should lie down," I said, putting my arm around his shoulder. Without arms, his body felt slight and somehow bereft.

"Thank you. I've had this cough lately, and pain in my chest." His body was stiff. We stood for a moment as the bee buzzed around our feet. Eventually, as if summoning up its courage, it made a quick circle around our heads and flew away.

There were patches of sunlight in the garden, but the dormitory was dark. Only the windows caught the light, sparkling brilliantly. Somewhere, behind one of those windows, someone had disappeared; I was here on the porch, rubbing the Manager's back; and my cousin was held up because someone had thrown himself in front of a train. There was nothing to connect these three facts, but for some reason they had melted together in the reflection from the window.

The Manager finally caught his breath. "Could I ask a favor?" he said. "Would you mind coming with me to look at his room?" The request seemed so odd that I hesitated. "I go there from time to time," he continued. "I keep thinking we must have missed a clue. Maybe you'll notice something, seeing it for the first time."

He was still having trouble breathing. I told him I'd be happy to go with him.

But I didn't find anything, either. It was a perfectly ordinary dorm room, with a desk and chair, a bed, and a chest of drawers. It wasn't particularly neat and clean, nor was it messy. The traces of the student's life had been left just as they were. The sheets were wrinkled and a sweater was draped over the back of the chair. A notebook filled with numbers and symbols lay open on the desk, as if he had got up from his studies for just a moment to go get something to drink.

The bookshelf held a mixture of travel guides, mysteries, and books on mathematics. The calendar on the wall was still turned to February, with notes jotted down here and there—"Ethics paper due," "Seminar Party," "Tutoring"—and above a line drawn from the fourteenth to the twenty-third, "Ski Trip."

"What do you think?" the Manager said, glancing around the room.

"I'm sorry," I said, without looking at him. "I see the room of a normal, well-rounded student, but I can't tell much more."

We stood for some time without speaking, as if we thought the missing student might suddenly reappear if we waited long enough. Finally, the Manager spoke again.

"He disappeared on the thirteenth, the day before he was due to go skiing. He was so excited about the trip. He was learning to ski, and I suppose he was just getting to the point where it was fun. When I told him I liked to ski myself, he wanted to know all about how I did it—what kind of boot I wore on my fake leg, how I held the poles. There was something very innocent and childlike about him when it came to things like that."

I ran my finger over the square marked "13" on the calendar. The paper was cool and rough. A pair of skis was propped against the bookshelf, still in their cover. A ticket for the overnight bus to the ski slope was tucked into the pocket of his bag.

"There was something special about the fingers of his left hand," the Manager said. His gaze was fixed, as if he were trying to recapture the image of the boy that lingered in the room.

"His left hand?"

"That's right. He was left-handed—he did everything with his left: combed his hair, rubbed his eyes when he was tired, dialed the telephone. He also made delicious coffee, and he often invited me in for a cup. We would sit together right here." As he said this, the Manager sat down in the swivel chair at the desk. His leg made a loud creak.

"He would show me how to solve math problems. Simpler ones that anyone would find interesting, ones that had to do with everyday life: how a mountain as huge as Mount Fuji could be reflected in something as tiny as an eye, how to move an enormous temple bell with your little finger—things like that. I had no idea that you could use math to figure out that sort of thing." Though I was still standing behind him, I nodded and he went on.

"He'd always start by saying, 'It's pretty simple if

you think about it this way . . .'; and no matter what kinds of naïve or stupid questions I asked, he never lost his patience. Actually, he seemed to love the questions. He always had a sharp pencil in his hand, and he'd scribble down numbers and symbols as he explained what formula he was using and why. His handwriting was rounded and neat—very easy to read. And in the end, a simple solution would appear, as if by magic. 'Pretty interesting, isn't it?' he'd say, smiling at me as he underlined the answer."

He took a deep breath before continuing.

"When he sat there with his pencil in his hand, he seemed to be spinning a beautiful web rather than just writing numbers. The strange mathematical symbols he wrote were like delicate little works of art, and even the regular numbers seemed extraordinary. I drank his coffee and listened to his explanations, and the whole time I couldn't take my eyes off of the beautiful fingers on his left hand. They were constantly in motion, as if moving made them happy. It wasn't a particularly masculine hand. The fingers were pale and slender—like exotic hothouse flowers. But each part seemed to have its own expressive quality—as if the nail on the ring finger could smile, or the joint of the thumb was shy."

His tone was so passionate that I could only nod. I looked once more at the things that had been left in the room—the pencil sharpener and the paper clips and the compass that the boy's pale fingers must have pinched and rubbed and held. The notebook on the desk looked expensive but well worn. It occurred to me that the wrinkles in the sheets would probably never be smoothed out, the sweater never put away in the drawer, the mathematics problems never completely solved.

The Manager began to cough again. The sound was so forlorn that I thought for a moment he was sobbing. The cough echoed in the empty room.

The next day I went to the library to learn more about the boy's disappearance. It was a small branch library in one corner of a park, the kind of place children go to find picture books. But they were able to get me all the newspapers from February 14, and I went through the articles in each local edition. The papers formed a sizable stack on the table in front of me.

There had been various noteworthy incidents that day. A housewife who had been painting her bathroom had died after being overcome by fumes. An elementary school student had been found trapped inside a refrigerator that had been left at a garbage dump. A sixty-seven-year-old man was arrested for swindling women he had pretended to marry. And an elderly

woman was taken to the hospital after eating hallu-
cinogenic mushrooms. Apparently, the world was full
of complicated matters that I'd never dreamed of, but
all these horrible misadventures were little more than
fairy tales to me. What mattered at the moment was
the boy's beautiful fingers.

No matter how much I read, however, I made little
progress with the mountain of newspapers; and no
matter how many articles I scanned, I found no mention of those hands. My own fingers were black with
ink and my eyes were stinging. There were any number of poisonings and asphyxiations and swindles, but
nothing to point me in the direction of the boy. I could
tell from the light coming in the window that the sun
was going down.

I don't know how long I was there, but at some
point a man carrying a large ring of keys appeared in
front of me.

"We're closing soon," he said, sounding apologetic.

"I'm sorry," I said, gathering up the newspapers. It
was pitch black outside.

When I got home, there was a letter from my husband. The bright yellow envelope, the foreign woman
on the stamp, and the unfamiliar letters on the post-
mark all reminded me that the letter had come from
someplace far away. It was hiding at the bottom of the
postbox.

The letter was long, with a detailed description of the large house where we would live in the small sea-side town in Sweden. There was a market on Saturday mornings where you could get fresh vegetables, and a bakery near the station that made delicious bread. The sea, which was always stormy, was visible from the bed-room window, and squirrels came to play in the garden. It was a very pastoral sort of letter. And then on the last page there was an itemized list of things he wanted me to do:

1. Renew your passport.
2. Get an estimate from the moving company.
3. File a change of address form at the post office.
4. Go to say good-bye to the boss.
5. Go jogging every day. (You need to be in shape—it's damp and cold here.)

I read the letter several times, stopping here and there to reread a line and then going back to the be-ginning when I reached the end. But somehow I couldn't really understand what he was trying to say. The words—"market," "squirrel," "passport," "moving company"—were like obscure philosophical terms. The formulas written in the missing boy's notebook seemed much more real to me. The notebook held the reflection of the steaming coffee, the left hand, the Manager's watching eyes.

There was something irreconcilable between Sweden, wrapped up in the yellow envelope, and the Manager, coughing pitifully in his room at the dormitory; and yet they were together. There was nothing to do but put the letter in the back of the drawer.

Ten days later I went to check on the Manager again. This time I took custards. My cousin was off in the mountains at a handball camp.

It was raining after a long dry spell. The Manager was in bed, but he sat up as I lowered myself into a chair. I put the box of custards on the night table.

The Manager seemed even thinner than usual. I rarely noticed the empty spaces where his arms and leg should have been, but as he lay motionless in bed, the lack was inescapable. I sat watching him until my eyes began to ache from staring at nothing.

"How are you feeling?" I asked.

"Well enough," he said, smiling weakly for a moment.

"Have you been to the hospital?" I asked. He shook his head. "I don't mean to pry, but shouldn't you go see someone? You seem to be in a lot of pain."

"You aren't prying," the Manager said, shaking his head.

"I have a friend whose husband is a doctor. He's a dermatologist, but I'm sure he could give us the name of the right specialist. And I'd be happy to go with you."

"Thank you," he said. "It's good of you to be so concerned. But I'm fine. I know my own body."

"You're all right, then?" I said, pressing the point. "You'll get over this soon?"

"I'll never get over it." His tone was so matter-of-fact that I didn't understand at first. "It will keep getting worse. It's an irreversible condition, like late-stage cancer or muscular dystrophy. But in my case it's simpler. I've been living all these years in this unnatural body, and now it's just wearing out. It's like the rotten orange in the crate that ruins all the good fruit around it. At this point it seems to be my ribs—they're caving in on my heart and lungs."

He spoke slowly and deliberately, as if trying to avoid adding to the pain in his chest. At a loss for words, I stared at the raindrops making their way down the windowpane.

"I did go to see a doctor at one point," he continued. "One of the students who lived in the dormitory went on to become an orthopedist. He showed me the X-rays he'd taken. Have you ever seen an X-ray of your chest? Normally, the ribs are symmetrical, and the heart and lungs fit neatly inside. But the X-ray showed that my ribs are bent out of shape, like tree branches that have been hit by lightning. And the ones around my heart are the worst of all—it looked as if they were about to pierce right through it."

The Manager took a breath and tried to compose himself. His throat made a rasping sound. A silence settled between us, and I counted the raindrops on the window, gliding down one after the other. When I got to fifty, I looked back at him.

"Isn't there something they can do to keep the ribs from caving in?" I asked.

"It's too late," he said, without any hesitation. "They said it would help a bit if I lay quietly on my back, but there's not much they can do."

"What about surgery?"

"No operation can bring back my arms and leg, and as long as I have to do everything with my chin and collarbone and this one leg, my ribs will continue to contract."

"So there's nothing to be done?" I said. The Manager blinked instead of answering.

The rain continued. At times it was so fine it seemed to have stopped, but when I looked carefully, I could see that it was still falling.

Pale lavender tulips were blooming in the flower bed. Every time I came to visit, the tulips were a different color. The moist petals glistened like mouths smeared with lipstick. And as always, bees were buzzing around the flowers. I found myself wondering whether bees normally came out in the rain, having no recollection of having seen them on stormy days. But these were definitely bees.

They flew here and there in the rain-streaked garden. One would disappear from sight, high in the sky, while another flew down in the tangled grass. They were constantly in motion, but for some reason each one glistened brilliantly, and I could see every detail, down to the delicate patterns on wings so fine they seemed about to dissolve.

The bees would hesitate for a moment before approaching the tulips. Then, as if making up their minds, they came to rest on the thinnest edge of a petal, their striped abdomens quivering. The wings seemed to melt in the rain.

As we sat silently in the Manager's room, the buzzing seemed to grow. The thrumming, which had been muffled by the rain, became more and more distinct, filtering into my head like a viscous fluid seeping through the tubes of my inner ear.

Suddenly, a bee flew in through the open window above the veranda and came to rest on the spot in the corner. The spot had grown again and stood out vividly against the white ceiling. I was just going to ask about it when the Manager spoke.

"There is something you could do for me," he said, as the sound of the bee's wings died away.

"Anything at all," I said, putting my hand on the bed where his right hand would have been.

"Could you get my medicine?"

"Of course," I said. I took a packet of powder from the drawer of his nightstand and filled a glass from the pitcher of water that had been left by his bed. Everything he might need—the telephone, a box of tissues, the teapot and cups—had been brought from elsewhere in the apartment and arranged close to the bed. The change was minor, but to the Manager it must have seemed as though his world was shrinking along with the space in his chest. I watched a drop of water fall from the lip of the pitcher, and a chill went down my spine.

"I hope this helps," I said, trying to appear calm as I tore open the packet of powder.

"It's just to make me more comfortable," he said, his face expressionless. "To relax the muscles and soothe the nerves."

"But isn't there anything they can do?" I asked again.

The Manager thought for a moment. "As I've told you, the dormitory is in a period of irreversible degeneration. The process has already begun. It will take some time yet to reach the end—it's not a matter of simply throwing a switch and turning out the lights. But the whole place is collapsing. You may not be able to feel it; only those of us who are being sucked in with it can. But by the time we understand, we're too far along to turn back."

As he finished speaking, he tilted his head back and opened his mouth. It seemed delicate and almost feminine. On the undersides of the soft lips, two rows of even teeth were lined up like carefully planted seeds. His tongue was curled back in his throat.

I poured the powder into his mouth in a thin stream. Then he took the glass between his chin and collarbone, just as he had always done, and drank without spilling a drop, and I thought about his pitiful ribs, about the X-ray of translucent bones aimed at the heart.

Another letter came from my husband: "How are your preparations coming? I haven't heard from you, and I've been worried." There were more descriptions of Sweden: the supermarkets and the vegetation, museums and roadways—sunnier than in the last letter. And at the end, as before, was an itemized list of my "homework":

1. Contact the telephone company, the electric company, the gas company, and the city about the water.

2. Apply for an international driver's license.

3. Check into the tax code for overseas residents.

4. Reserve a storage unit.

5. Gather up as much nonperishable Japanese food as possible. (I'm beginning to get tired of the salty, tasteless food here.)

If you added these to the ones in the last letter, I now had ten tasks to complete. I tried reading them out loud to put them in some sort of order, but it didn't help. I had no idea how to prioritize or where to begin in order to get to Sweden.

I put the letter in the drawer and took out my quilting. I had no particular need now for a bedcover or a wall hanging, but I couldn't think of anything else I had to do.

Blue checks, and then black and white polka dots. Plain red, and green with a pattern of vines. Squares, rectangles, isosceles triangles, and right triangles. The quilt grew, but as I sat there in the stillness of the night, sewing patch after patch, I suddenly heard the thrumming of bees; and the sound, no matter how faint, would not go away.

I began to go to the dormitory every day to look after the Manager, and each time I took a different treat:

madeleines, cookies, cream cakes, chocolates, yogurt, cheesecake. At last I got to the point where I had no idea what to take. The tulips bloomed, the bees buzzed, the stain on the ceiling grew larger, and the Manager, with each visit, grew rapidly weaker. He stopped going out to shop, and soon he was unable to prepare his own meals. He began to have difficulty feeding himself or even getting a drink of water, and, finally, he was barely able to sit up in bed.

I went to take care of him, but there wasn't much I could do. From time to time I would make him some soup or rub his back, but for the most part I simply sat in the chair next to his bed. His ribs were slowly caving in on his body, and I could only sit and watch.

It was the first time I had ever nursed someone, and the first time I'd seen someone deteriorate so quickly. It frightened me to think how things would end if he went on this way. I became unbearably sad when I imagined the moment his ribs would finally pierce his heart, or the weight of his artificial leg as it was removed from his cold body, or the deep silence in the dormitory when I was left all alone. The only one I could count on was my cousin, and I found myself praying he would come home soon from his handball camp.

That day, it began raining in the evening. I was feeding the Manager the pound cake I had brought him. He lay in bed, the covers pulled up to his chin, staring off into space. From the way the blanket rose and fell, it was obvious that he was having trouble breathing. Pinching off bits of cake in my fingers, I held them near his mouth. His lips parted only slightly, and when I had slid the cake in, he held it there without chewing, as if waiting for it to dissolve. Over and over, he pecked at bits of cake until the slice was gradually consumed. My thumb and index finger were shiny with butter.

"Thank you," he said, a bit of the cake clinging to his lips. "That was delicious."

"I'm glad you liked it," I said.

"Food actually tastes better when someone feeds it to you." He lay on his back without moving, as if his body had been stitched to the bed.

"I'll bring something else when I come next time."

"If there is a next time," he said, though the words were little more than a sigh. Unsure how to respond, I pretended I hadn't heard him and stared at the butter on my fingers.

I realized it was raining. The tulips in the flower bed were trembling and the bees' wings were damp. The tulips today were a deep blue, as if someone had spilled a bottle of ink on them.

"What an odd color for tulips," I murmured.

"I planted them with the boy who disappeared," the Manager said. "He came home one day with a bag of bulbs. He said he'd picked them out of the trash bin in back of a flower shop. They were tiny things, and I didn't think they'd amount to much. . . ." His pupils shifted to look out the window. "But he was absolutely convinced they'd bloom. He dragged an old desk into the courtyard and laid out the bulbs on it. He divided up the different varieties and figured out how to fit them all in the flower bed. The plan came to him in an instant, and it turned out to be exactly right. He seemed to have a knack for that sort of thing. It was probably because he was a mathematician, but it still impressed me. There was a different number of bulbs for each color, but he came up with a way to fit them all in the bed, without a single one left over."

The evening shadows crept in from the corners of the room. The box of pound cake on the kitchen table disappeared into the darkness. The Manager looked away from the window and continued his story.

"We let the bulbs dry in the sun for a few days and then went out to plant them. No one had done anything with the flower bed for a long time, so the soil was as hard as a rock. He sprinkled it with the watering can and then broke it up with a tiny shovel, the kind kids use in a sandbox. It was the only one we had. He did everything with his left hand, of course, and in no time we had a bed full of rich, beautiful soil."

I sat quietly and listened.

"Finally, we were ready to plant. He dug shallow holes in the pattern he had worked out. Then he would put a bulb on his left palm and hold it in front of me, and I would push it in the hole with my chin. His hand was as beautiful covered with dirt as it had been holding a pencil and writing down numbers. The sunlight glistened on his palm, his fingers had red marks from the handle of the shovel. He held the bulbs cupped in his hand, and each time I brought my chin close, the pain in my chest was almost unbearable. The pattern of his fingerprints, the pale veins, the warmth of his skin, the smell—everything oppressed me. I held my breath and tried to hide these feelings as my chin nudged the bulb into the hole."

His gaze was fixed and unblinking as he finished his story. He sighed and shut his eyes, asking if I would let him rest awhile.

It was growing dark. The white sheets on the bed seemed to glow between us. The rain continued to fall, swallowed up by the darkness.

His breathing became slow and regular, and he fell gently off to sleep. I looked about at the objects in the room—the clock on the wall, the cushions, a magazine rack, the penholder—waiting for my eyes to adjust to the low light. Everything was still and quiet, as if it had fallen asleep with the Manager.

But in the silence, my ears suddenly sensed a vibration, and I knew instantly that it was the bees. It was a steady hum, a fixed wavelength. If I concentrated, I thought I could even hear the sound of wings rubbing together. It was a low, heavy sound, too deep to be confused with the rain, and it breathed inside me now, a monotone chant sung by the dormitory itself. Outside the window, the tulips and the bees faded into blackness.

Then a drop fell at my feet. It fell slowly, right in front of my eyes, so that even in the dim light I could sense its size and density. I looked up at the ceiling. The round spot had sprouted arms like an amoeba and had spread over my head. It had grown enormously and had begun to bulge down from the ceiling. Drops fell in a steady rhythm from the center.

"What could that be?" I murmured. I could tell that the liquid was thicker and heavier than the rain falling outside. It lay beaded on the carpet without sinking in.

I called quietly to the Manager, but he didn't answer. The wings buzzed in my ears as I reached timidly toward the drops. The first one skimmed the tip of my finger, but, summoning up my courage, I pushed my hand into the stream. The next drop landed in my palm.

It was cool. I sat with my hand frozen, wondering whether I should wipe the sticky drop with my handkerchief or crush it in my fist. More drops fell, one after another.

I stared at the pool accumulating in my hand, but I could not tell what it was. The Manager was asleep, my cousin was away at his camp, and the mathematician had vanished. I was alone.

The boy who solved math problems with a pencil, who planted bulbs with a tiny shovel—where had he gone? Drip. Why were the tulips such strange colors? Drop. Where was my cousin? Drip. How did the Manager know so much about my cousin's joints and muscles?

My hand felt heavy and numb. The pool grew in my palm.

"Blood?" I said aloud, though I could barely hear my voice over the hum of the wings.

Blood. So this is how it feels. I'd never seen it so fresh. I once saw a young woman hit by a car. I was ten, on my way home from the ice-skating rink. Blood was everywhere—on her high heels and her ripped stockings and all over the road. It was so thick it seemed to form little mounds—just like this.

I shook the Manager and called his name.

"Wake up!" I screamed. There was blood on the blanket, on the toes of my slippers. "Wake up! Please!" I called again.

I shook him harder, but his body had become a

dark lump on the bed. He was so light I could have picked him up, but I couldn't wake him no matter how much I shouted.

But it was my cousin I was worried about. I wanted to see him again, see that shy smile and the way he poked at his glasses. I knew I had to go look for him now.

Groping my way from the Manager's room, I ran up the stairs. The lights were out, and night had crept into every corner of the building. Ignoring the sticky film on my hands and feet, I ran down the hall, breathing hard, my heart pounding. The sound of the bees filled my ears.

My cousin's door was locked. I grabbed the knob with both hands and tried to force it open, but I only managed to make it sticky.

I ran on to the mathematician's room. This time the door opened immediately, and I found everything exactly as it had been when I visited with the Manager. The skis and the bus ticket, the discarded sweater and the math notebook—everything was waiting quietly for his return. I looked in the wardrobe and under the bed, but it was no use. My cousin wasn't there.

I knew at last that I had to go look above the spot on the ceiling, to find out where the drops were falling from. The thought came to me with sudden clarity, as if I'd come to the important line in a poem. I went back down the stairs and found a flashlight in the shoe cupboard in the lobby. Then I went outside.

My hair and clothes were wet by the time I had crossed the courtyard. The rain was fine, but it settled over me like the strands of a chilly spider's web.

I gathered some empty crates that were scattered around the courtyard and stacked them under the Manager's window. I was wet and alone and teetering on a pile of boxes, but I was oddly calm. I had the feeling that I had somehow been lured into this unlikely predicament, but I tried to remind myself that it would all be over soon and the world would return to normal.

Above the window was a rusted grate covering an opening to the crawl space between floors. I pulled it free, and it dropped to the ground with a dull thud. The boxes swayed, and I clung to the window for a moment. I looked up, and the rain fell on my eyelids, on my cheeks and throat. My fingers were slippery, but I managed to turn on the flashlight and shine it into the crawl space—illuminating an enormous beehive.

At first, I didn't realize what it was. I had never seen a beehive so close. It lay over on its side in the long, low space, and it was unbelievably large, like an oddly shaped fruit, swollen all out of proportion. The surface was crusted with tiny lumps, overlaid with a tracing of fine lines. It had grown so huge that it had begun to split open in places, and honey spilled from the cracks, dripping slowly and thickly, just like blood.

The sound of wings filled my ears as I stared at the hive. I reached out for it. The honey flowed on, somewhere beyond the tips of my fingers.